**"You said it was somebody's birthday. So I brought over some Buckton brownies."**

Cooper looked genuinely surprised. From behind him came the smiling face of a young girl. Then came an odd clicking sound as crutches came into view, flanking the ruffles of a frilly party dress. Tess told herself not to stare as the ruffled skirt ended in only one white cowboy boot.

"Sophie, this is the lady who told me about Lolly's blondies," Cooper said.

Sophie's eyes grew wide. "They were super yummy!"

Tess felt herself smile. "Another of my favorites is my grandmother's brownies, and she insisted I bring some over to the birthday girl."

"I'm six now," pronounced Sophie. She shifted to show off her solitary boot. "Do you like 'em? They're my birthday present."

There was something brave and bittersweet in how the child referred to her single boot as a pair. "Mighty nice," Tess said. "White boots are extra special—you must be extra special yourself."

She'd called a little boy in Adelaide "extra special"—a little boy she'd never get to buy birthday presents for now—and the words sat bittersweet on her tongue.

**Allie Pleiter**, an award-winning author and RITA® Award finalist, writes both fiction and nonfiction. Her passion for knitting shows up in many of her books and all over her life. Entirely too fond of French macarons and lemon meringue pie, Allie spends her days writing books and avoiding housework. Allie grew up in Connecticut, holds a BS in speech from Northwestern University and lives near Chicago, Illinois.

## Books by Allie Pleiter

### Love Inspired

#### Blue Thorn Ranch

*The Texas Rancher's Return*
*Coming Home to Texas*
*The Texan's Second Chance*
*The Bull Rider's Homecoming*
*The Texas Rancher's New Family*

#### Lone Star Cowboy League: Boys Ranch

*The Rancher's Texas Twins*

#### Lone Star Cowboy League

*A Ranger for the Holidays*

#### Gordon Falls

*Falling for the Fireman*
*The Fireman's Homecoming*
*The Firefighter's Match*
*A Heart to Heal*
*Saved by the Fireman*
*Small-Town Fireman*

Visit the Author Profile page at Harlequin.com for more titles.

# The Texas Rancher's New Family

## Allie Pleiter

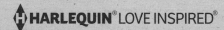

Recycling programs
for this product may
not exist in your area.

LOVE INSPIRED BOOKS

ISBN-13: 978-0-373-89951-7

The Texas Rancher's New Family

Copyright © 2017 by Alyse Stanko Pleiter

www.Harlequin.com

Printed in U.S.A.

But he said to me, "My grace is sufficient for you, for my power is made perfect in weakness." Therefore I will boast all the more gladly about my weaknesses, so that Christ's power may rest on me.

*—2 Corinthians* 12:9

To Linda

Because she's stronger than she knows

# Chapter One

"Just one—no, two." Tess Buckton ogled the covered dish of Lolly's Diner's decadent blondies, fighting the urge to buy all of them. After flying halfway around the world in the last thirty hours, she could easily eat the whole plate without stopping. Not that she would, but she could. "Okay, three. But no more."

"They that good?"

Tess's jet-lagged brain struggled to distinguish the Texas surroundings she stood in now from the Australian settings she'd left behind. It took a few seconds to recognize that the Aussie accent she'd grown so used to hearing didn't belong in her hometown of Martins Gap, Texas. She turned to see a tall, tanned cowboy, one eyebrow raised in question as a smirk turned up one corner of his mouth.

"Yeah," she said, "they are. I just got back into town and I've been dreaming of these since I got on the plane thirty hours ago. I've been in Adelaide, actually."

His eyes widened at the mention of the Australian city. "From near Alice Springs, up in Northern Territory, myself. Not that you could tell from the accent, I'm sure." His smirk spread into a full-blown and rather disarming smile.

Her brother Luke had mentioned this guy in an email. There had been talk of the well-known Australian horse trainer looking at the property abutting her family's ranch. According to Luke, some said he was renting it for the season, others speculated he was planning to buy the land at the end of the summer. "I'm guessing your last name is Pine," she offered.

The man put one hand on his chest. "Guilty as charged."

One of the famous Pine brothers. Only, which one? She looked at him, trying to draw the face of either of the TV celebrity siblings up from her sleep-deprived memory. It wasn't like she'd ever really followed the show, but it was famous enough that ads for it were pretty much impossible to avoid.

"I'm the other one," he said, tipping up his hat.

She laughed as she accepted the bag of three blondies from Lolly and immediately reached into the bag for one.

"That would make me Cooper," he explained. She nodded as she bit into the confection, glad not to have to admit she could only remember Hunter Pine's name in her present state. He cocked his head toward the other four blondies still remaining on the covered plate. "There's a little lady at my house with a birthday tomorrow. Should I buy the rest?"

Luke hadn't mentioned that the man had a wife in his last email. Only that the rumors had been true and one of the famous Pine brothers had indeed showed up and moved into the vacant ranch house—but for how long? Her brother was wondering about the answer to that question, and so was she. A tiny town like Martins Gap wasn't really the kind of place she expected someone of Pine's notoriety to put down roots.

"Yes," she answered him, "I'd stick a candle in any one of these." Tess sent an appreciative smile Lolly's way. Lolly's blondies were the ultimate comfort food for her, and she could use a whopping dose of comfort these days. "They're as good as I remember."

"Of course they are, Tess, honey," Lolly replied.

"Tess? Tess Buckton?"

"That's me." Gran would scold her for forgetting to introduce herself, but Gran hadn't been up for thirty hours and multiple time zones.

"We're neighbors," Cooper said as he pointed to the remaining blondies and then held up four fingers to Lolly. "I'm renting the Larkey place for the season. Beaut land."

"Wish I could say as much for the previous owner," Tess replied the moment her mouth wasn't full of gooey white chocolate and caramel. The cowboy's charming but clearly amused smile made her wonder just how much powdered sugar was all over her blondie-craving face. Tess wiped the last of the powdered sugar off her fingers against her jeans and shook Cooper's huge tanned hand. "Pleased to meet you."

"I keep hearing things that tell me this Larkey bloke wasn't pleased to meet anyone. But I hear good things about Bucktons. I should have known you were part of the clan. The eyes and all."

Most Martins Gap residents knew the

Buckton family for the bright turquoise color of their eyes, but she didn't really expect the reputation to extend to seasonal renters of foreclosed properties. "So you're here for the summer?"

"Yeah. Layin' low a bit."

Tess looked at the delicious square in her hand and debated whether downing an entire blondie in front of a complete stranger would constitute the best first impression.

Her expression must have been a dead give-away, for Cooper nodded toward the blondie and said, "Go 'head. Don't lemme stop ya."

She did. She wanted to eat all three in rapid succession, even knowing that would make her nearly ill by the end of it. Lolly's blondies. She'd been craving them every day since she'd booked her flight. Now she could eat them every day for as long as she was here—which might be a while. She took another bite as Lolly handed her the change from her purchase. As the woman lifted the lid on the cake plate to remove the remaining four, Cooper snatched one and took a healthy bite.

"Oh," he said from behind a mouthful. "I see your point. These will definitely make her day."

Lolly beamed but she didn't exactly look surprised. And why should she? Tess couldn't recall a single person who didn't love Lolly's blondies. If Martins Gap had an official dessert, this was it. Even Gran—who was famous for her own brownies—admitted that Lolly topped her efforts.

"So, you're just staying for the summer?" Tess asked as she put her wallet back in her handbag. She wasn't usually the type to fish for gossip but his comment had practically handed the opening to her. And she had to admit, she was curious.

Cooper smiled, pointing to his mouth now full of a second massive bite of blondie. Tess waited for him to finish but, even though he'd talked right through his last bite, he never offered an answer, just a dramatic "Mmm-mmm" as he paid Lolly. As if he'd never heard her question.

He finished the transaction, tipped his hat with a dashing wink at both Lolly and Tess, and headed out the door...

And practically headlong into Luke, who had gone to visit his fiancée's physical therapy practice in town while Tess got her blondie fix. The frost between the two men could be felt even from this distance. No words passed between them as Cooper walked away.

"You ready to head to the ranch?" Luke

asked, still staring at the doorway Cooper had exited. "Gran'll be waiting."

*Gran.* Tess swallowed the conflicting feelings that rose around the prospect of seeing her grandmother again. So much in her life had changed in the sixteen months since her last visit and she was crawling home in a defeat no one yet knew had come. On the one hand, Tess yearned to spend time with the wise, tenderhearted woman who had raised her after her mother's death. Next to Luke, Tess had felt closest to Gran when their mother's death had turned her eleven-year-old world upside down.

It was Gran and Luke who had been her anchors in the nine years her father had lived after that, nine years her father hadn't made pleasant for any of the four Buckton children. Dad was the reason all of them had left the ranch and Gran was the reason each of her siblings had returned, one by one, in the past few years.

But Gran could always read her almost as well as Luke could. Which meant one of them was bound to figure out what had happened and why she was back. She could hope to keep the events of recent months from one of them for at least a little while, but both of them? She didn't stand a chance.

*You knew that when you chose to come home*, she told herself. Not that there had been all that much choice to it. What was the saying? Something about how home is the place where, when you have to go there, they have to take you in. And she'd had nowhere else to turn.

"Tess?" Luke peered at her, thrusting his face into her vision, snapping her thoughts away from halfway around the world to another time and place. "You hungry or something? I mean, hungrier for more than blondies?" After a second, when she didn't answer, he added, "You okay?"

"I've been up for thirty hours, that's all. I didn't conk out on the plane like I usually do." As well traveled as she was for her job as a freelance photographer, Tess usually made excellent use of red-eye flights. Only these days Tess didn't sleep well no matter where she lay her head—and that had nothing to do with jumping the international date line.

"All the more reason to get you home so Gran can fuss over you. Catch you later, Lolly." Luke gave a wink—as much of a showman's wink as the one Cooper Pine had given—to the woman behind the counter and plucked the bag from Tess's hands as they headed for the door. "You got one for me, didn't you?"

"Would it matter if I didn't?"

He pulled open the bag. "Only two cleaned Lolly out?"

"No, I got three, but Cooper Pine cleaned her out of the other four."

"Cooper Pine," Luke muttered behind a mouthful of blondie. Her brother spoke the name with a distinct lack of Texan hospitality. Which was amusing, because from what she'd heard of the Pine brothers, Cooper and Luke had loads of attention-grabbing showmanship in common. "I hoped he was only vacationing, but I told you rumor has it he's thinking about buying the place."

"I tried to ask him about that, but he didn't answer. Deliberately dodged the question, I'd say."

Luke grunted. "Why'd the bank rent to him anyway? Don't foreclosures usually sit empty? The last thing we need is to look down our drive and see a line of Pineys camped out in front of his gate."

Fans of the horse training program known as the Pine Method—"Pineys," they liked to call themselves—existed in Australia and Texas, and probably every other city the brothers visited on their popular, televised training tours. Their methods often achieved amazing results, but that was only half the reason for their celebrity. The way Tess saw it, the brothers' stunning good looks, their dynamic personalities and the sheer relentlessness of their marketing had done the rest. Pineys were mostly female and it wasn't hard to see why.

Having grown up on a ranch, Tess had as much appreciation of an attractive man who looked at home on horseback as the next girl. But that didn't mean she was ready to get caught up in the hype. Tess didn't own a horse, and even if she did, she wasn't sure she would count herself among the Piney ranks. Their expensive videos, weekly television series, multiple books and vast selection of Pine Method merchandising struck her as a bit over the top.

"Did you tell him you'd just come from Australia?" Luke asked, driving with one hand while he polished off the blondie with the other.

"I did."

"Did he go all 'G'day' and 'Down Under' on you, dialing up that fake charm? Honestly, he acts like he thinks we've never seen an Aussie before."

Luke was a fine one to talk about being an

overbearing flirt. Before the rodeo accident that ended his bull-riding career, Tess would have clocked Luke in as possessing more ego than both Pine brothers combined. "I think he's married. Did you know that?"

That seemed to surprise her brother. "I didn't. Wouldn't surprise me, though—the ladies seem to go for him, and he must pull in a pretty paycheck. I haven't seen her. Now that I think of it, I barely see him."

"And yet you're sure he goes all Aussie on everyone." This was a case of the pot calling the kettle black. Or at least, it would have been before—for the old Luke. She was rather impressed with the person her twin brother was becoming lately. Luke—formerly a confirmed and rowdy bachelor who couldn't imagine any life outside of the razzle-dazzle of the rodeo circuit—had settled comfortably back in their hometown and was getting married to his high school sweetheart. This was not only good news, but offered Tess a convenient excuse to come home from halfway around the world.

"Have you ever met an Aussie before Cooper Pine?"

Luke grunted. "'Course I have. A few were on the bull riders tour. Dated a few sheilas, too."

Tess knew enough Aussie slang to find the term for females ridiculous in Luke's Texan drawl. "More than a few, I imagine. All of that being over now, of course."

"Of course."

"Because Ruby knows how to make you pay if you get too friendly with any of those Pineys who might be lining up near home."

"Ugh, what an awful thought. Not Ruby— but a bunch of screaming fan girls scaring the herd. No one wants him and his crazy brother to put up a Buy Your Show Tickets Here billboard." Luke pulled onto the road that led up toward the Blue Thorn Ranch. The familiar scenery began the slow, peaceful seep into Tess's soul. The house with its sprawling front porch. The barn. The green of the pastures with the ever-growing herd of bison silhouetted against the blue of the sky. *Home. For now or for good? I'm still too hurt to know that yet.*

"Still, anyone's got to be an improvement over Larkey, right?" The ranch's former owner had caused serious trouble for their oldest brother, Gunner Jr., as the Bucktons had fought to keep the Blue Thorn Ranch from the clutches of a shady land developer awhile back.

"You'd think," Luke replied. "Can't say as

I'm sure yet. For a brother act like the Pines, we've only seen Cooper. Hunter hasn't shown up yet—so I'm taking that as a good sign." Hunter was the dominant brother of the pair, if the advertising was to be believed.

Of course, the advertising also made both brothers look very single and available. They presented themselves as rugged bachelors, which made the information about Cooper's "little lady" a surprise. Was the omission privacy or just careful marketing?

"He seems nice enough."

Luke glared. "You been here, what—all of an hour? And you've decided our close-mouthed new neighbor is 'nice enough'?"

Tess put the snarky remark down to soon-to-be-groom stress and hauled herself out of the pickup to take in the glorious sunshine that only the Blue Thorn Ranch could offer. For better or worse, she was home.

Cooper placed the bakery bag down on the kitchen counter. "Glenno," he called to the longtime employee who had managed his house no matter where he lived, "what time is it in Alice Springs?"

"Seven tomorrow morning," came Glenno's voice from inside the pantry. The kitchen of this place was large but outdated. Cooper made a mental note to himself that he was going to have to push out the back wall to make a dining room big enough for his plans.

Plans he'd have to reveal sooner or later. He could do it now, while his brother Hunter was back home taping a special Outback segment before their next set of Pine Method tour dates. Sure, it'd be the coward's way out to tell Hunter his plans while the man was halfway around the world, but he'd chickened out all the other times Hunter had been close by. He knew he needed to get it over with…but Sophie's birthday was tomorrow and he had no desire to spoil the celebration by igniting that particular bomb today. Or was he just making excuses for himself again?

"Hunter's up," Glenno said as he came out of the pantry with a bag of onions, "if that's what you're thinking." The man had always been so much more than just a cook or house manager—he was a wise part of the family. He was also the only other person who knew Cooper's plan. For the hundredth time since renting the ranch, Cooper wondered how long it should stay that way.

"He called half an hour ago," Glenno added. He smiled as if that were a trivial detail, as if the strain between Hunter and Cooper was simply a ripple on a much larger pond. For a man continually dragged around the world in the wake of his famous employer, Glenno was the happiest man Cooper knew. "At home in his own skin everywhere," Hunter used to say.

The call wasn't a trivial detail, because his brother was never known to be an early riser. The early hour either meant Hunter was losing his famous immunity to jet lag, or he was itching to share some new business plan for the Pine Brothers' franchise. Given Hunter's nonstop drive, it wasn't hard to guess which.

Cooper shared neither his brother's drive, nor his travel immunity. He'd skipped this latest jaunt back Down Under on the half-truthful premise of wanting a between-season break, but it was really more than that. He needed time to think about how to dismount the constant media carousel that had been his life for the past few years.

How do you tell your brother you still want to be brothers but not part of the Pine Brothers?

You don't. Or, at least, you drag your feet on doing so. Heaps. "Why didn't Hunter call my cell?"

"He did," Glenno answered wearily. "Only, since it was sitting on your desk, it wasn't much help."

Despite owing much of his success to the technology that allowed the media to promote him around the clock, Cooper hated cell phones. If he had his way, he'd never carry one. He hated how the thing took up all the space in his pocket and assumed he'd pay it nonstop attention. There was a time a man could be alone with his thoughts in the world, not feel compelled to type them continuously into cyberspace with itty-bitty keys or even just pictures of keys.

Hunter, of course, owned a smartphone, two tablets and one of those new watch gizmos to boot. The man had been known to post videos of his lunch to social media. Even if Hunter was in the remotest quarter of the Outback, he was never off the grid and never off the stage.

Cooper ignored Glenno's long-suffering look, pointing instead to the white paper bag. "A new recipe for you to figure out. But save one for Sophie to have tomorrow—those things are delicious." Glenno, aside from being a great cook, was also somewhat of a gastronomic sleuth, forever attempting to recreate sauces, dishes and foods he found in restaurants or shops. If Glenno's track record could be trusted, Cooper and Sophie could have an unending supply of Lolly-like blondies whenever they wanted them by the end of the week, if not for tomorrow's birthday.

Then, casually, Cooper added, "I met another of our neighbors today."

Glenno began inspecting one of the blondies with a scientific squint. "More Bucktons?"

"Yes. At least this one's pretty."

Glenno smirked. "So not Luke or Gunner." He broke off a corner of the treat and tasted it. After a moment's savoring, he gave an approving nod. "Very good. Who'd you meet?"

"Tess. I'd heard Luke had a twin, but I always assumed it was another bloke. This sister just blew into town—from Adelaide, believe it or not. Why didn't anyone tell me one of the Bucktons was there lately?"

Glenno broke off another piece. "Because they don't talk to you. Because you don't talk to them. Because they're afraid this ranch is about to become another stop on the tour and you don't tell them otherwise." He set the confection down. "You can't start if you don't start."

Another Glenno-ism. The man had an unending collection of wise sayings that didn't quite make sense. Hunter called him the Aussie Yogi Berra—something Glenno took as a compliment. "I just have to find a way to tell

Hunter first. Word might spread, and I don't want him to hear it from anyone but me."

Glenno took a piece of the blondie, sniffed it then squished it between his fingers, testing the texture. "You keep waiting for the perfect time to tell your brother unwelcome news. The longer you wait, the worse the news gets."

"Not if I tell him the right way." But Cooper knew his voice lacked conviction. They'd had this conversation a dozen times already.

Glenno shook his head. "Even if you tell him the perfect way." He looked at Cooper. "You want to do this thing, dontcha?"

From the moment his plan arrived in his head, seemingly straight from God Himself, Cooper had never wanted to do anything more than the plan he was waiting to launch right now. "Of course."

"And you know Hunter won't approve."

"I think that's pretty much certain, don't you?"

Glenno nodded once. "Two facts that won't change no matter how much time you let them sit. But the sooner you tell him, the sooner you two can start working past this. He is your brother, mate. Give him some credit for wanting you to be happy—once he has a chance to get used to the idea."

Cooper poured himself a cup of coffee. "Credit? Remember what's going on here. I'm breaking up the act. Hunter's going to take that like a stab in the heart. He won't just say 'goodonya' and move on like it's just a minor ding. I'm denting—maybe even sinking—the Pine Brothers' brand. The unforgivable sin. I doubt he'll ever speak to me again after I tell him."

"And yet you keep saying you're tired of Hunter deciding your future."

"Daddy! You're back!" Cooper heard the welcome sound of his very nearly six-year-old daughter coming down the hallway toward the kitchen. "I need your help." He turned to see Sophie's face scrunched up beneath two wild peaks of strawberry-blond curls. "I can't do it. You hafta." She leaned her crutches up against the kitchen counter and slid onto the seat next to him, catching sight of the white bag as she did. "What's in there?"

Break out early birthday blondies? Or make another sad attempt at Daddy pigtails? It wasn't a hard decision. "Special six-year-old birthday goodies that were supposed to be for tomorrow. But they can arrive a day early for anyone having pigtail troubles."

She grinned up at her father. "That's me."

"They're called blondies, and a lady in

town said they were her absolute favorite. I knew right then I needed some for my little lady on her birthday." Glenno produced a plate, and Cooper slid one of the goodies onto it and in front of Sophie. "I've barely mastered the ponytail, sunshine, and now you want two?"

"And braids."

Cooper laughed. "I'm pretty sure braids are beyond me."

"Oh, Daddy," Sophie said after a hearty "Mmm" to go with her first bite of the confection, "nothin's too hard for you. Not even French braids."

Cooper looked at Glenno. "What's a French braid?"

Glenno smirked. "Harder than a regular braid, I expect."

Sophie unleashed her hair from the uneven tangles and placed the glittery holders on the counter in front of Cooper. "I want to wear pigtails on my birthday tomorrow. Can't you try? Please?"

Cooper had watched his fair share of how-to videos just to master the ponytail—an irony not lost on a horse trainer. Still, all those curls atop a wiggly five-year-old, combined with the challenge of maneuvering those impossibly tiny elastics, made two pigtails feel nearly impossible. Still, this was Sophie. How could he say no?

"I'll look it up tonight and we'll give it a whirl tomorrow." He thought about Tess Buckton, the pretty neighbor he'd just met. She had long hair. Maybe he could override his "keep to yourself" rule in the name of birthday hair.

Then he remembered Luke Buckton's none-too-neighborly glare as he'd left the bakery.

Maybe not.

## Chapter Two

The next morning, Tess pulled a Blue Thorn Ranch truck up to the main house after being buzzed in at the Larkey ranch. She'd have to stop calling it that if Cooper stayed. It had been the Larkey ranch—often said with a derisive sneer for the wily, backstabbing former owner—for her whole life. Well, lots of things were changing around here. The loss of Larkey as a neighbor could only fall into the positive column as far as she was concerned.

She adjusted the basket on her arm and rang the doorbell on the big, beautiful old home. A startling squeal—a distinctly little-girl sound—came from inside the house. Could it be that Cooper Pine's little lady really *was* little? The thought surprised her as Cooper's face peered through the door's small upper window before he pulled the door open. "Well, hello there."

"You said it was somebody's birthday. Blondies—even Lolly's—aren't enough for a birthday in my book. So I brought over some Buckton brownies." She held out the basket. "Welcome to the neighborhood."

"Well," Cooper said, looking genuinely surprised, "look here. Buckton birthday brownies."

From behind him came the smiling face of a young girl—eyes as green as her father's, but with a wild tousle of strawberry-blond curls rather than Cooper's darker hair. Definitely Cooper Pine's daughter. Was she the birthday girl? Or was it her mother, whom Tess thought was probably back somewhere in the house—maybe in the kitchen, munching down a blondie?

Then came an odd clicking sound as a pair of Canadian crutches came into view, flanking the ruffles of a frilly party dress. Tess told herself not to stare as the ruffled skirt ended in only one white cowboy boot.

Cooper was clearly accustomed to smoothing over such moments for his daughter. "Sophie, this is the lady who told me about Lolly's blondies."

Sophie's eyes grew wide. "They were super yummy!"

Tess felt a smile spread easily to her face. "I know. They're among my favorites. But another of my favorites is my grandmother's brownies, and she insisted I bring some over when she learned there was a birthday girl in the house today."

"I'm six now," pronounced Sophie with regal emphasis. So the birthday was hers. "That means I go to first grade in the fall." She shifted on the crutches to show off her solitary boot. "Do you like 'em? They're my birthday present."

There was something brave and bittersweet in how the child referred to her single boot as a pair. Tess liked her immediately, feeling guilty for her momentary stumble. "Mighty nice," she said. "I've always felt white boots were extra special. Never had white ones myself—you must be extra special."

She'd called a little boy in Adelaide "extra special"—a little boy she'd never get to buy birthday presents for now—and the words sat bittersweet on her tongue.

Sophie, oblivious to Tess's memories, somehow executed a twirl on the crutches. It flounced her ruffled skirt out in girly splendor. "Thanks. Daddy says so all the time."

Still no mention of a "Mommy." And this "Daddy" was not the Cooper Pine of the Pine Method empire or the man with the gleaming toothy smile from the television show. His off-camera persona was quieter, calmer, less imposing, but still in full possession of the charisma she imagined made him a star. And probably won him the heart of some strawberry-blonde who had given him this beautiful daughter. So where *was* the mother? The noise and chatter at their doorstep would have sent most women Tess knew out to see what was going on.

"Good for Dad," she said. "I don't mean to interrupt if you've got a party planned."

"Can you braid?" the little girl asked.

"Huh?"

Sophie tugged on her curls. "Braid. Hair."

Cooper shrugged. "I'm kind of out of my league here, and someone wants birthday braids."

But wouldn't her mother...? Oh, Tess thought with a momentary shock of understanding, remembering being a little girl herself with no mother to fix her hair anymore. Apparently this precious child was Cooper's one and only little lady, after all.

Tess stared down at those sweet eyes. "Birthday brownies and braids, that's me."

"Well, then," said Cooper as he gestured her inside, "come on in. As a matter of fact, your timing is downright great. Glenno will want to know if we got the blondies right, and you're just the taste-tester we need."

"You're right!" Sophie cheered, suddenly taking off down the hallway in a tumbling three-legged canter that Tess had to admire. "Glenno! Glenno!" Her cries echoed as she disappeared to another part of the house.

"Our cook, among other things," Cooper explained as he relieved Tess of the basket. "I call Glenno our culinary lyrebird. Likes to figure out other people's recipes and imitate them. I gave him one of the blondies yesterday." He looked down at the basket. "Um… these aren't a secret family recipe, are they?"

Tess felt a little knot pull at her stomach. "As a matter of fact…"

Cooper pulled open a door on a hallway credenza and slipped the basket in. "I'll hide 'em for now. Later, Sophie and I will dig in on the sly." He tapped the door shut with his cowboy boot. "No point baiting Glenno's curiosity."

Tess heard the *click-click-clop* of Sophie's boot and crutches long before the girl popped up from around a corner down the hall. "Are you coming yet? Glenno thinks he got it on the first try."

Tess threw a sideways glance to her "host."

"I doubt Lolly will be happy to hear that."

The resulting grin *did* belong on a charming television star. "I won't tell if you don't."

By the time Cooper led his short-order hairstylist to the kitchen, Sophie was seated on one of four stools in front of a kitchen island, her crutches dispatched to a nearby corner. She spun on the stool's swivel seat, her leg swinging in anticipation.

"I've got a niece not too far from your age at Blue Thorn, you know," said Tess. "You'd like Audie."

*A friend?* Cooper pondered the possibility. His travel schedule hadn't afforded Sophie many chances to make friends—one of many things he was set to change—and one just across the road would be a blessing. All Sophie really needed was one soul her age who would see past the crutches to the treasure that was his darling daughter.

"Miss Tess," Sophie said in an amusingly formal tone, "this is Glenno. He's kinda everything."

"G'day to you." Cooper watched Glenno chuckle at the "job description" as he extended a hand in greeting. "From the Buckton place, eh?"

Cooper had heard bits and pieces of the past tension between the former owner of this property and the Buckton family. Sophie neither knew nor cared about such neighbor relations. She simply grabbed the plate from one end of the counter and pulled it toward the middle open stool. "Taste 'em."

Tess's glance bounced among Copper, Sophie and Glenno before she sat. "They *look* like Lolly's," she offered, tilting a smile toward Sophie's eager eyes. Actually, Glenno's eyes looked just as eager.

"But do they *taste* like Lolly's?" he encouraged, sitting beside Tess so that she was between him and Sophie. "That'd be the million-dollar question."

With all three sets of eyes fixed on her, Tess picked up the square and had a bite. It seemed like ten minutes went by, even though Cooper was pretty sure it had only been seconds, before she smiled.

"Mr. Glenno, I think you lived up to your reputation."

Glenno beamed. Sophie giggled happily. The tension Cooper had felt tighten his chest all day in how he was going to give Sophie the best day he could unwound a bit at the culinary victory.

"These are ninety-nine percent Lolly's. And I couldn't rightly say that the lacking one percent isn't just pure loyalty to Lolly." She took another bite as Sophie leaned in to watch.

Cooper made a big show of absconding with one of the blondies from the plate and began eating.

"Hey!" Sophie cried out. "No fair. I can test again, too, can't I?"

As if he could deny Sophie anything on her birthday. Cooper slid the plate toward her while Glenno gave a grunt of victory and picked up the last confection. For a moment everyone ate in blissful silence. Cooper sent a prayer of thanks heavenward for the tiny, spontaneous party.

"You can't tell her you've done this," Tess said eventually. "I love Lolly too much to let her know you've figured out her recipe."

"I promise you," Cooper said, not bothering to hide his grin, "she'll never know."

"I'd never undercut the woman who made these," Glenno said. "I'm not out to get anyone. I just like the challenge."

"I just like the results," Cooper said as he licked his fingers.

"I just like the eating," Sophie said, sending them all into laughter. "Glenno, you're the best. You should do Miss Tess's brownies next."

Tess shot Cooper a look. Cooper shot his daughter a look. "Sophie, hon, I promised Miss Tess we wouldn't let Glenno swipe her grandma's recipe."

"Brownies?" Glenno looked intrigued and put out at the same time.

"I saw Dad hide 'em in the hall cabinet." Sophie pronounced. "Want me to go get 'em?"

She began to slide off the stool until Cooper popped up and snatched the crutches out of her reach. "We'd better have another little chat about the virtues of discretion."

"Dis-what?"

"Not telling secrets that aren't yours to tell," Cooper explained. "What do I always say?"

"Everybody doesn't need to know everything." Sophie turned back around and plunked her elbows on the counter. "But you love Uncle Hunter and you say he likes everybody to know everything."

*Proving my point exactly.* Sophie was a little sponge, picking up on everything he said whether he liked it or not. "I do love Uncle

Hunter. But I don't always agree with him. Brothers are like that."

"How would I know?" Sophie had been on a rant lately about not having siblings. He hated how lonely her childhood had been. He had good reasons to keep her from the Pine Method fans and fans from her, but that made for more seclusion than Grace would have ever wanted for their daughter.

Grace, God rest her soul. He seemed to miss his late wife more than ever these days. Back when it had been the three of them, their family unit had felt perfect and complete. But now he was constantly aware of just how thoroughly he'd let Grace carry the burdens of parenting—and how inadequate he was to handle it without her, even with Glenno's help. There just weren't enough hours in a day to be the Pine Method professional the world expected him to be and the father Sophie needed him to be at the same time.

And it wasn't like there was other family to turn to. Hunter had no interest in domesticity and with Grace's parents halfway around the world and his own folks gone, family was in short supply. Cooper didn't really feel connected anywhere.

And that was going to change. He pulled Sophie into a hug, ruffling the curls that were so much like her mother's. "You don't know, that's why I'm telling ya." It was one of the reasons he was trying to get off the Pine Brothers' tour so he could make a go of settling down somewhere good for her. It had been different when she was very small and Grace was around, but hopping from tour to tour with Glenno and him was proving no way to grow up.

"Do you have brothers, Miss Tess?"

"Two of them. And a sister, too." She'd caught on to Sophie's pout, for she added, "They're not as much fun as you think some of the time."

"Miss Tess here's a twin."

As diversionary tactics went, it was a fine one. "No fooling! Does she look just like you?"

Tess laughed. "I hope not. My twin is my brother Luke. My older sister, Ellie, she's having twins and they'll be a boy and a girl, too. Luke and I are going to be their godparents. They'll be here in June, and I'm sure they'll be cute as buttons." She turned her eyes to Cooper. "Will you be here in June?"

"We'll be here forever," Sophie cut in.

He really needed to watch what details he gave that girl—or at least make her understand which ones to keep to herself. They still needed to play this close to the vest until he could get over the hump of extracting himself from Hunter.

"Forever?" Tess repeated. She'd caught the split-second exchange of glances that flashed between him and Glenno. "So you *are* buying?"

Sophie said, "Yep!" at the same time Cooper said, "Maybe."

How to cover that? Cooper wasn't foolish enough to doubt his secrecy led to speculation within the Texas community. It was perfectly reasonable for folks to think this ranch would simply take its place on the Pine Brothers' tour the way Hunter's ranch north of Houston had. Clearly, the Bucktons wouldn't be lining up to buy tickets.

This would all be better once he told Hunter. He just had to play it quiet until he could settle it within the family. Then he could exit the show and move forward with his plans to open a therapeutic horse ranch for kids like Sophie

For now he just nodded at his daughter and said, "How about those braids now?"

# Chapter Three

"So…" Ellie said as she eased her swollen frame next to Tess on the overstuffed wicker couch on Gran's front porch the next day. "What's Cooper Pine like?" Ellie and her husband, Nash, had a house in town near the office where Nash was sheriff, but on days when Nash was on duty Ellie often came out to the ranch house where Gran loved to fuss over her very pregnant granddaughter.

"I'm just taking care of my girl," Gran would always say—even though at eighty-five Gran ought to start letting other people take care of her. Some days it was hard to judge which woman's body gave her more grief; swollen Ellie or aging Gran.

"He's nicer than he looks on television," Tess offered.

Gran gave a scandalous wink. "That must

be pretty nice. Those Pine brothers are some fine-looking men. Good horse trainers, too," she added when Ellie rolled her eyes.

"His little girl is darling," Tess explained.

"So he's not married—or not married any-more—but a single dad?" Ellie asked. "How come no one knows about his little girl?"

Fishing for the right words to explain the girl's situation, Tess offered, "I hope it isn't her disability. She doesn't seem to let the fact that she has one leg slow her down a bit."

"One leg?" Gran's eyes popped. "Like an amputee?"

"I don't know," Tess answered. "She was wearing a frilly dress long enough that it was hard to tell anything beyond the fact that there was only one boot and that she walked with crutches. I didn't think it was right to ask. She wasn't wearing a prosthesis, though, and it certainly wasn't a new injury. She was faster than me on those things."

"I had no idea," Ellie said. "Like I said, they never mention a daughter on the show. Yes, I watch," she admitted when Tess gave her a look. "I have to spend a lot of time off my feet these days and they're entertaining when they bicker. Reminds me of Luke and Gunner."

"Or Luke and you, for that matter," Gran

said to Tess. "There were days I thought you two would skin each other alive the way you fought. Did you find out his plans for the place? Is Gunner right to be worried that it will become some tourist attraction?"

Tess thought about the way Cooper had dodged her questions about his long-term plans. "Sophie said they would be there 'forever,' but he only said a very vague 'maybe.' Why hide plans no one would object to? I got the clear impression he isn't eager to tell anyone what he's up to."

"Well, he hasn't bought yet." Gran stirred her iced tea and looked out over the Blue Thorn pastures. "That gives us some time to figure out what's going on."

Tess followed her gaze, seeing the ranch with fresh eyes after being gone for as long as she had, traveling around the world on freelance photography assignments for a collection of travel guides. Over a hundred bison now roamed the grassy stretches Gran and Grandpa and then Dad had worked when the Blue Thorn was a cattle ranch. Gran had a right to be fiercely protective of what happened around the Blue Thorn. Bucktons had fought long and hard for generations to keep this ranch up and running, and no one wanted it to become the sideshow to a Pine Brothers' publicity circus.

Gran set down the glass. "We should get to know him. It's the right thing to do, and useful besides. How old did you say his girl is?"

"Six as of yesterday. Although she reminds me of Audie—a lot smarter and more mature than her years. I get the feeling nothing gets by that girl."

"Even better. You go on back over there tomorrow, bring them some bison burgers, and invite them to supper Saturday. Audie won't have school so the two girls can meet, and we can throw us a barbecue like he's never seen."

Tess laughed. "They barbecue in Australia, Gran. They barbecue in Korea, for that matter. And he's spent a fair amount of time in Texas. I think he's seen barbecue."

Gran grinned. "Not ours. The man's already tasted my brownies—how could he possibly turn us down?"

Tess envisioned Glenno dissecting Gran's brownies behind Cooper's back and just gave her grandmother a sigh. A second unannounced visit to Cooper and Sophie? Would that look odd? It wasn't like they had a phone number she could just call. She was pondering about how to word her invitation when she became aware of silence on the porch, and Gran's eyes fixed on her. "I'll go over there tomorrow."

"That's fine and dandy, but let's talk about you." Gran picked up her knitting—a baby blanket in cheery blocks of turquoise and white. Ellie was working on a sweater of the same color combination from her spot on the couch. "I'm glad you're back, but you still haven't really said why."

"I'm home to see Ellie's twins being born. To do the whole godparent thing with Luke. For Luke and Ruby's wedding. There are plenty of reasons to be here, so why wouldn't I visit now?"

Ellie shifted her weight on the couch. "You came home with four suitcases and two cameras. This isn't a visit." After a moment Ellie added, "Is it?"

How could she give an answer she didn't yet know herself? It was so, so good to be home and yet at the same time, she didn't know what her place was here anymore. Her other siblings had settled so thoroughly into the running of the ranch and its side businesses. Where did she fit? Tess felt like the missing piece in a nearly finished puzzle— everything else was in its place but her. "I'm staying through the wedding, but I don't know my schedule after that."

That was a very sketchy way of glossing over the fact that she'd sold all the rest of her equipment and her furniture, walked out on an apartment lease and didn't have new work lined up. "I don't know my schedule" was miles away from "my life is in total collapse because of what happened in Adelaide."

Gran let the knitting fall to her lap. "Don't get me wrong, sugar, I'm thrilled to have you back on the ranch. I just get the sense there's more to why you're here than babies and weddings. I know you. You won't tell me till you're good and ready. But I just want you to know I'm ready to listen when the time comes."

She'd have to tell them eventually. Gran was right—she always did in the end. But sharing this story would be harder than anything she'd ever had to confess before. She'd loved sending back reports from exotic places all over the world, swooping in for short stays where she could dole out bits of news at her own speed. The months she'd spent in Adelaide had turned her life upside down—in both good and bad ways—and she hadn't yet come up with the words to tell even these people—who loved her—what had transpired. Both intertwined stories were long, emotional tales, and she couldn't find the words to start the telling. Or to whom.

Should she confide in Luke, who knew her best despite their long estrangement, which had now ended? Gunner, who'd become such a wise leader of the family she hardly recognized him from the rebellious teen who'd left before their father died? Compassionate Ellie, who knew what it was like to have a relationship go sour on a grand scale? Or Gran, who would never judge no matter what Tess revealed? Gran would understand how you can love in an instant for no good reason, how someone can yank the foundation out from under your life in ways you never saw coming.

She could start with Gran, but not here and not now. This had to go in bits and pieces, one bit at a time—only she couldn't figure out which bit to tell first. For a split second Tess thought it might be easiest to tell Audie, whose "soul was far beyond her years" as Gran used to say. But Audie was far too young to hear about how people you thought you loved could rob you blind.

Tess thought about Bardo. How could she ever explain the way her heart had moved when she'd looked into the little boy's sweet brown eyes? How he'd told her his name meant "river"? How the orphan's sadness clung to her in a way she knew would never subside? Four was far too young to be so old and sad. She thought back to yesterday, when she'd seen Sophie all dressed up for her birthday and radiating happiness at her presents. Watching that little girl's joy only made her ache for the little boy from the Australian foster home she'd met on a photo shoot.

He'd stolen her heart in a single afternoon. Tess had started visiting every week, then twice a week, then every other day. The fierce craving to be Bardo's mother—something that made no sense and was for all practical purposes nearly impossible—came out of nowhere. The Aussie foster home system worked so well that orphan adoptions of any kind were all but nonexistent. Less than one hundred per year to Aussie families. A twenty-five-year-old, single, American woman didn't stand a chance. How could she explain how she'd thrown herself and all of her savings into trying anyway? At the urging of a man she thought loved her but turned out to just want her money? The failure felt too big to speak. Too humiliating to share, even with the people who loved her best.

*I came home to family because all of a sudden I need to be a family but can't. Because*

*I lost a lot of money trying. Because Bardo needs my love and I need his but a thousand rules and regulations won't ever let that happen. Because I've been fooled by a man I never should have trusted. Because I'm deep in debt and grieving for something I never had and can't ever have. I have to figure out what's next, but I haven't a clue where to go from here.*

Gran's eyes softened as Tess realized her eyes burned with tears. The old woman reached out and squeezed Tess's hand—a wordless comfort for a wordless plea.

"I've got some things I need to work through." She fumbled the words out, afraid if she said more the whole story would come rushing out of her before she was ready.

Gran gave her hand another squeeze and offered a sad smile. "Don't we all, child. Don't we all."

Cooper looked up from some landscaping sketches to peer out his office window at the sound of a vehicle coming up the drive. Who would...?

At the same time he heard Sophie racing down the hall. "Dad, Miss Tess is back!"

He'd told Glenno not to let just anybody in when the intercom buzzed—but he was hard pressed to say this interruption bothered him. Still, why was she back?

Sophie appeared in his study doorway, grinning. He was an introvert, craving his privacy, but clearly Sophie took after her extroverted mother. Her face fairly lit up at the prospect of company. "Well, you ought to go get the door then, girlie." He stood as Sophie took off toward the front door.

She practically squealed her hello to poor Tess. He was relieved to hear Tess laugh at the enthusiastic greeting—Sophie was a bit much at times, but he loved her exuberance. He'd always thought it God's gift to a little girl who'd have to scale a mountain of obstacles in life. When he made it to the front door, Tess and Sophie were sitting on a hallway bench while Sophie peered into a brown paper bag.

"What'cha got there, Sophie?"

Sophie looked up with wide eyes. "Bison burgers." She thought for a moment then asked, "What's a bison?"

He knew the Blue Thorn Ranch had been revitalized from a failing cattle ranch into a thriving bison ranch by Tess's older brother Gunner. "It's another name for a buffalo."

Sophie looked at Tess. "You can eat 'em? How do they taste?"

"Delicious. You can eat their meat, you can wear their hides, you can even make yarn out of their coats." Tess leaned in. "You just can't pet them. Or ride them."

That made Sophie giggle. He'd pointed the huge brown animals out to Sophie on the rare times they'd gone off the ranch together and some of the Buckton family's animals stood near the road that separated their ranches.

"Actually, I'm rather glad you haven't met them yet. There was a time when a few of our bison were known to wander over to this land. The former owner used to get rather steamed about it."

Another reason Paul Larkey wasn't everyone's favorite neighbor. Would that help the case for what he wanted to do when he shifted from tenant to owner of the ranch? Or hurt it? *You have to buy it from the foreclosure bank first, which means you have to tell Hunter first,* he reminded himself. "Nope," he offered. "We've not had any bison come to visit that I know of."

"You've got a lot of open land here," she said. "Larkey used to raise cattle, but I expect you know that."

She was polite enough not to go on to "So what are you going to raise?" but it was clear she was thinking it. It made him wonder what prompted today's visit. Was this a Buckton family fact-finding mission?

He must have scowled because she got to her feet. "I came with an invitation."

"And bison burgers," Sophie added as she handed the bag to Cooper and maneuvered to her feet.

Cooper was impressed that Tess didn't try to help Sophie up. Sophie could do most things for herself, and was never shy about asking for help if she needed it. Anyone who treated his little girl like every other little girl won points with him. "An invitation?"

"To dinner Friday night. You and Sophie and Glenno, if he promises to keep quiet about any recipe swiping. And…anyone else here."

Was she fishing to see if there was a Mrs. Pine? "Just the three of us." In truth, clients would eventually visit on therapy days, but he opted out of mentioning that complication. Two months ago it felt like he couldn't breathe word of the equine therapy services he wanted to provide, but he was slowly feeling an urge to let it out. Hunter had to be the first to know—but it sure would be nice to hear someone else say, "You're not crazy. An equine therapy ranch is a good thing, and you should do it."

"Well," Tess replied to his earlier comment, "then we'd like 'just the three of you' to come to supper Saturday night."

Cooper had to ask, remembering the suspicious looks Luke had given him in Lolly's not two days ago. "And your brothers are okay with this?"

"It was my grandmother's idea, and Gran trumps everyone on the Blue Thorn. Besides, I think getting to know each other is a better idea than throwing each other frosty looks in town, don't you think?"

So she had noticed. And it felt like she was on his side. Cooper wasn't prepared for how that wrapped itself around him. His much-lauded instincts told him she wasn't being nice to him just because he was Cooper Pine. It startled him how refreshing he found the realization.

Sophie dragged him from his thoughts by tugging on his arm. "Can I go bring these to Glenno? Can we have them for lunch?"

"Sure thing." He watched her clip down the hall before turning to Tess. "Thanks for the burgers. And the invite."

"You're welcome."

There was an odd, stretched-out moment where they realized they were alone together with nothing much to talk about. Tess shrugged and looked around the great room behind them. "You know, it's not at all like I pictured it."

"How's that?"

He walked ahead of her into the room. The space had too much dark wood in it—the place needed lightening up in a million ways—but there was a solidness to the property Cooper could see under all the dated fixtures. When the rental manager had showed him the place as "a real bargain," he'd had this inexplicable sense of him needing it and it needing him. Not that he'd ever voice anything so odd.

"We used to make up stories about the inside of this place when I was growing up." She looked at the room with just a hint of the long-lost feeling he'd had at his first look.

It couldn't be her first look—she'd grown up across the road from the place, hadn't she? "You mean you've never seen the inside of the house before?"

"Dad and Mr. Larkey were never friends. My brothers and I used to dare each other to see how close we could get to this house before old man Larkey chased us off. Gunner told me he saw hunting trophies through the windows once, and we made up stories about how he got them."

"There were two or three on the walls when I got here. I took them down before Sophie arrived." He looked around the room, finding it still too dark and bare for the place Sophie would grow up.

"She'll love Martins Gap. Sure, we've got some of the small-town gossipy stuff going on, but you'll find most folks will take to her like ducks to water." She turned to him, evidently deciding to be direct. "I'll warn you, those burgers and the supper invitation come with strings attached. My family really wants to know what your plans are."

That was no surprise. "Texans are a neighborly lot, but two visits in four days tells me *y'all* are seriously curious." He used the colloquialism as a joke, but as soon as it was out of his mouth he realized it sounded absurd in his accent.

"Just so you know, you'll be grilled Saturday night." She went on. "In the most polite way possible, but grilled none the less. I figured it was fair to warn you."

"Consider me warned," he replied as he opened the doors that led out to the patio. She'd made a gesture on her part, he ought to do the same. "So I'll say this. I've got plans under consideration. I'm just not of a mind to share them yet." He tucked his hands into his pockets. "Will that be enough?"

She raised one eyebrow. "I doubt it." She exhaled and sat on the low stone wall that surrounded the patio. "But I get what it's like to not be ready to tell the whole world all your plans. The need to keep secrets. But my brothers are going to make it hard on you. You shouldn't blame them—they've fought hard to keep the Blue Thorn going and to make it a success, and they're afraid whatever you've got planned might be a threat."

Cooper sat in one of the old wooden chairs that had been left with the property. "So you came to feed me, invite me and warn me?"

She smiled. "Well, yes. You should also know I think Audie could be a great friend to Sophie, and it'll help if Gunner's not suspicious of your motives."

He stretched his legs out, crossing one boot over the other. "And what does Gunner think my motives are?"

"Honestly?"

"Straight up, mate. I've probably heard it all before anyway."

Her back straightened. "He's worried he'll wake up one morning to a full-blown Piney fan festival out his front window. He thinks you'll be bringing the whole TV thing here, complete with crowds and fuss."

"That I'll open a souvenir shop in town next to the Blue Thorn Store where he sells his stuff?" he continued, fully aware he was pushing her buttons. "How would that be different from what your family already does? Wouldn't both offer products to the public that support a family ranch business?"

"I wouldn't put a single store selling bison meat and yarn in the same boat as a franchise pitching arena shows, DVDs and T-shirts." When he raised an eyebrow she added, "We don't have a fan club."

"So everyone expects me to be the showman Hunter is."

"And you're not?"

She had him there. He hadn't given them any reason to think he didn't share Hunter's obsession with a high profile.

Still, that didn't make his brother the bad guy here. He wasn't even involved in what this ranch would become—even if he didn't know that yet. "Hunter is my brother. I owe lots of what I have to him and what he's done."

He didn't quite hide the unspoken "but..." tacked on the end of that thought. She evidently knew a dodge when she saw one.

"Is he your partner in this? In whatever it is you're thinking of doing here?"

He'd heard the Bucktons were stubborn, but he hadn't expected Tess to be this relentless. And she was the one who seemed to be on his side! Just what was he in for on Saturday?

"I know you don't *owe* us an explanation," she said, softening her tone, "but it would help things if you told us what you *aren't* doing here if you can't tell us what you *are* going to be doing."

Cooper didn't like being pushed, but he also didn't like starting off on the wrong foot with people who would be his neighbors and hopefully friends to Sophie. He pulled in a breath then let it out slowly. "You've got nothing to worry about."

She frowned. "That's not much to go on."

"It's not anything I want made public. At least, not yet. So that's the best I can do. Even at a barbecue."

"Well, I'm not going to take back the invitation, if that's what you're thinking. You're still invited. And warned." She paused for a second before offering him a startling smile, completely out of place given the tension of their conversation just now. "I hope you'll come."

# Chapter Four

Cooper's second thoughts Saturday morning did not meet with Sophie's approval. His daughter looked as if he'd plunged a knife through her tiny little heart when he suggested declining the Bucktons' barbecue invitation. "Of course I want to go to the party!" she whined, draping herself across the couch in pint-size devastation. If he put his foot down and begged off, he'd have a miserable night here, that was clear. "I wanna go," she moaned, limbs stricken akimbo in flailing disappointment. "I *hafta* go."

Cooper began picking up the pieces of the game they had been playing. "You don't *hafta* go anywhere. And it's not a party. It's just a supper." A supper he doubted would be much fun for him, at least, even if it meant seeing Tess Buckton again. Then again, Sophie would meet Audie, and that was worth enduring the "grilling" Tess had said was coming, wasn't it?

"It's a barbecue. A bison barbecue. I've never been to one before." One hand lay across her forehead in such a drama-queen pose Cooper wondered what movies she'd been watching. "And now I'll never go."

He tried to swallow his reluctance as he slid the lid onto the game box. "I know you like Miss Tess and all…"

"I love Miss Tess. I wanna meet the little girl at her ranch. She'd said we'd like each other." Sophie didn't have to actually say "and now you're taking it all away" because her eyes screamed it at him. "Why'd you hafta fight with her?"

"We didn't fight."

Sophie sat up and crossed her arms over her chest. "She didn't seem very happy when she came in the kitchen to say goodbye."

"We had a discussion. Maybe a difference of opinion, but not a fight. That's different." He pointed at Sophie. "Just like you and I are having a difference of opinion right now."

Sophie's chin practically sank itself into her chest. "No, we're fighting. Miss Tess invited us to a party and you're saying we're not going. Did she take her invitation back?"

Cooper made it a point never to lie to Sophie, which made her ability to ask just the wrong question all the more exasperating. Tess had, in fact, reiterated her invitation despite their tense discussion. "No, she didn't, but it still won't be any fun if we go."

"It'd be fun for me," Sophie said softly. Her tone pinched his heart hard. What father wants to disappoint his daughter? She was right, though—it probably *would* be fun for her, even if it might end up torture for him.

She looked up at him with her "sad puppy eyes," her ultimate weapon against his willpower. Life had denied Sophie so much—a normal body, a mother to grow up with, family to surround her—he hated to be the one to deny her anything else.

"You really want to go?"

Clearly sensing he was weakening, she upped her game. In one move, she flung herself from the couch onto his lap. "More than anything. Pleeeeaaaasssseee can we?"

He knew that tone. The stubborn streak that got Sophie through the aftermath of her accident had a dark side, and he'd just landed in the middle of it. He'd hear that whiny request nonstop until he relented. Still, on things that really mattered, he could dig his heels in and be just as stubborn as Sophie.

But did this really matter? Could he tiptoe his way through a night of relentless Buckton questions if it meant Sophie could make friends with another girl near her age? It couldn't get that bad—no one would want to launch an argument in front of the kids. If he showed up a bit late and only stayed until Sophie's bedtime, surely he could stand it. *I've been stepped on, bitten, thrown, knocked over and kicked by the worst horses on two continents*, he reasoned. *How bad could half a dozen Bucktons be?*

"Okay, we'll go. Now go and see if Glenno's ready for you to help set the table." Glenno had rigged a special backward sort of backpack that allowed Sophie to carry plates and silverware to the table one at a time. It took much longer, but Cooper liked that Glenno was always quick to adapt the standard child chores to Sophie's abilities. Besides, the fifteen minutes it took Sophie to set three place settings was a bit of peace and quiet he sorely needed at the end of some days.

That peace and quiet was broken by rings from the telephone. Hunter's tone as he said, "G'day, mate," told him his unreturned phone call from earlier in the week hadn't gone unnoticed. "I know you're supposed to be on holiday, but have you got a minute for some good news?"

Cooper leaned back on the leather sofa. "Sure."

"The blokes in legal did a good job. We've got a signed statement from Lynette Highland. No more worries in that department. If she shows up anywhere near you, we have immediate grounds for a restraining order."

Cooper sighed. While he didn't want to talk about his future plans, he wanted to discuss this issue even less. "I'm glad to have that whole thing over with."

"You and me both, mate. What a circus that was."

Lynette was a production assistant—a very good, very pretty, production assistant—who had worked on the show. Three months ago she'd taken the very small inch of attention Cooper paid her and tried to run ten miles with it.

Making sure that Cooper had everything he needed was part of her job, and he'd barely noticed at first when she'd dialed up her attentions, constantly checking in with him and flirting all the while. When he had noticed, he'd been flattered and had allowed himself to cautiously flirt back, thinking a little dating might be nice. It had been the first time since Grace that a woman had even halfway appealed to him. Even Hunter had approved of Lynette as Cooper's "first wade back into the dating pool." They'd both been stunningly wrong—a Pine Brothers' first, to be sure.

The first date had been pleasant enough, but afterward her attentions toward him went from flattering to obsessive. Soon it had turned into a nightmare of phone calls, notes, far too intimate emails, even trying to show up at a hotel where he was staying on tour. He'd talked with Lynette. Hunter had sat with her. Even the producer very bluntly telling her she was endangering her job didn't seem to make a dent in her determination to win him over by every means available— without seeming to realize that all she was doing was frightening him away.

Lynette believed she had "found her meal ticket"—as Hunter began to put it—and didn't seem to think her job needed to matter much anymore. By the end, legal had had to step in and talk about a court order. The great blessing in it all was that sheer logistics—or God's mercy, as Cooper saw it—had kept Lynette from ever meeting Sophie. The whole business was the tipping point for Cooper's decision to leave the Pine Method.

"So now we can get on with the new season

without having any of that drama getting in the way. I gave the legal guys a 'good-on-ya' bonus for handling it quiet-like. That's not the kind of press any of us needs."

*The new season is already being planned? You can't wait forever, mate, you'll have to tell him soon. But "soon" doesn't have to mean "now."*

"No new season talk for a bloke on holiday. I'm glad for this news, but the rest can wait." He ignored the pang of guilt he felt for changing the subject. "What's this big surprise that's taking you so long to ship Sophie for her birthday?"

"Should be there soon. She's gonna love it."

Hunter had a flair for grand gestures that often defied common sense or, at least, parental wisdom. He relished his role as the indulgent favorite—if only—uncle, and had been known to go a bit overboard. There was a tricked-out, pink-and-purple ride-on Jeep on Hunter's ranch with "Sophie" painted on the side to prove it.

"Does it require safety gear?" It was only half a joke.

"Not a bit. Smaller than a breadbox, this one."

"What do they say about big surprises coming in small packages?"

"Relax, mate, you'll like this one. Although I'll say this much—it's something you'd never get her."

"Well," Cooper laughed, feeling a bit of the strain vanish between them, "that leaves the door wide-open."

"I'll be in on the eighteenth and we can catch up then," came Hunter's voice. "Gotta run—we're heading off to the last location in an hour. Kiss Sophie for me."

"Will do. 'Bye."

Cooper sat back after putting the phone down, a bit disappointed in himself for throwing away another opportunity to have his much-needed talk with Hunter—but still glad to know that whole business with Lynette was behind him. He ran his hands down his face, remembering the one mistake of a kiss. He'd been so careful up until then, knowing he was only on the outer edges of his grieving for Grace. He'd kept the loneliness at bay with business, but as Lynette had proved, it hadn't solved anything.

*Will it get worse or better out here, Lord? Help me be more careful. I can handle a problem like Lynette, but Sophie will latch onto anyone I let close.*

Anyone like Tess Buckton. Had she already gotten too close? Could he keep things within clearly defined margins where those intriguing blue eyes were concerned?

The barbecue might tell him soon enough.

Tess's cousin Witt Buckton raised an eyebrow as he handed a big package of bison burgers over the meat counter window. Officially in charge of the Blue Thorn Ranch's food truck that sold burgers and sides in downtown Austin, he wasn't at the Blue Thorn Store very often. Some of that had to do with his professional focus. A lot more had to do with the truck's pretty chef, Jana. Tess only had to see those two together for a handful of minutes at Ellie's wedding to know things had heated up in more than the truck's tiny mobile kitchen. The couple had married last August, and Tess had been sorry not to be able to make it back in for her cousin's wedding.

"Who's coming to supper?" Witt asked, noting the large amount of burgers she'd ordered.

"Cooper Pine and his daughter."

"I heard he's renting the old Larkey place, but I didn't know he had a family. Y'all getting a new neighbor?"

"It's anybody's guess. He says it's just him and his daughter for the summer. Gunner and

Luke think he's got plans—maybe to buy the place and make it part of the Pine Method franchise—but Cooper won't say. I warned him he'll get more of a grilling than the burgers, but he's coming anyway."

Witt laughed. "Brave soul."

"How's Austin's latest foodie power couple?"

Witt nearly glowed. "Will it sound dumb if I say ridiculously happy?"

Everyone within the Buckton family seemed ridiculously happy these days. Everyone except her, that is. It felt almost freakish to be nursing such private, painful wounds among all these gleeful relatives. "You've put on a few pounds," she teased. "Being married to a chef obviously agrees with you." The spark in Witt's eye clearly had to do with more than just good cooking.

He came out from behind the counter. "So, Ellie thinks you're back to stay—are you?"

It was a fair question, seeing how Gunner, then Ellie and then Luke had all returned to the ranch for good. Even Witt, who had grown up only visiting the Blue Thorn from his father's ranch, had chosen to join the Blue Thorn business. Still, the number of times she was asked that question was beginning to niggle under her skin. She tried to laugh it off. "I'm here for a stretch, between the twins coming and Luke's wedding. Beyond that, I don't know."

She fingered the selection of bison yarn gloves and scarves that hung on a nearby wall, evidence of how her sister Ellie had added to the family business. Now, Ellie was busy putting the final touches on baby blankets and booties. More happiness to envy and not have. She wouldn't ever be asking Ellie to knit scarves or hats for Bardo. Those joys would belong to his foster parents, not her. She planted a "happy auntie" smile on her face. "I'm in between assignments, so everything's up for grabs. Could be back to Adelaide, could be off to the Alps." That wasn't entirely true. She'd sold nearly all of her equipment to pay the adoption fees her adviser, Jasper Garvey, had required. Jasper had also made her believe he was helping because he loved her. She'd been ready to ditch her globetrotting lifestyle to settle down with Bardo, at whatever job would keep her in one place. She could try to roust up new freelance jobs and the equipment to cover her debts— and probably ought to—but that would take confidence and bravery she no longer felt she had.

Tess changed the subject. "I hear there's a

second big blue bus in the works?" Everyone teased Witt for the bright, almost eye-searing color he'd chosen for the food truck, but no one could deny it stood out, making it easy to spot—an important trait for a food truck in a competitive market.

His smile widened. "Launches in about a month. Jana says Jose is ready, and with Marny coming in the store full-time to fill in for Ellie, we're ready to expand."

Jose, who had been a protégé of Will and Jana's, was about to become a food truck chef in his own right rather than working with Jana as her assistant chef. Marny was a girl Ellie had mentored through a teen program at the church who'd had her share of problems but had made a way for herself thanks to Ellie and work at the Blue Thorn Store.

Gunner, Luke and Ellie were settled and happy. Not that they—or even Gran—hadn't known hard times. It was just that they'd all come shining through those challenges, and Tess couldn't clearly see that in the cards for her anymore.

"Are you and Jana coming tonight?"

Witt shook his head. "The truck's got to be downtown for an event. It'll be a hot date night in the hot kitchen, I'm afraid." His words spoke of work but his eyes beamed with the pleasure of working with his bride.

*I'm only twenty-five*, Tess told herself. *That's too young to feel like that will never happen for me.*

"Have fun tonight," Witt called as another customer came into the store.

"We'll have something tonight," Tess replied, recalling the tense nature of her conversation with Cooper Pine. "I'm just not sure it will be fun."

# Chapter Five

Tess had once had the opportunity to photograph a famous high-wire act. She'd been allowed up on the platform with the tightrope-walker, given access to the breathtaking perspective from way up high.

It rather felt like tonight's barbecue.

She was watching Cooper balance his way carefully through a barrage of questions, dancing over the heights of her family's barely veiled curiosity. Were it not for the instant friendship that sprung up between Sophie and Audie, she wasn't sure how the evening would have gone.

"Daddy didn't want to come," Sophie admitted as Tess and Audie gave her a tour of the barns and led her up to the fence that held Daisy and Russet, the only two bison on the ranch that were safe for human contact. "Safe human contact" was a relative term, meaning animals on one side of a very strong fence, humans on the other. But unlike the animals out in the pasture, it was possible to get close to these bison, and even to pet them, without spooking them.

*I can just guess he wasn't eager,* Tess thought. "But you're here." She made sure to say it with a smile.

"I convinced him after you had the different of opinion," Sophie pronounced, clearly quoting her father's words. She was either unaware of the level of her frankness or didn't especially care that she was revealing information Cooper probably didn't want Tess to know. She'd known Sophie for less than a week and was already one hundred percent charmed by the girl. As to her father? The jury was still out on him.

"Russet got his name from me on account of his color," Audie explained. "Bison babies are rusty colored when they are born. They only turn brown when they grow up." Audie leaned in toward Sophie. "Gunnerdad thought I was going to give him a girly name like Rainbow Sparkle when he let me name her."

"That's silly!" Sophie said as the pair of girls burst into laughter.

"He said nothing on his ranch would ever have that name," Audie shared through giggles.

The sound of two girls' laughter, even at the expense of her brother for his now-infamous worry over Audie's naming choice, melted Tess's heart. If joy had a sound, Tess thought it would be very much like those two right now. Did Bardo have friends to laugh with?

"What's so funny over here?" came Cooper's voice from behind them. "And who's this big fella?"

Tess let Audie, who never tired of introducing Daisy and Russet to guests, do the honors. "He's Russet," her niece said, pointing to the young male bison.

"Audie named him," Sophie offered. "And not Rainbow Sparkle." More giggles.

Cooper raised one eyebrow and scratched his chin. "I'm guessing there's a story there?" he said to Tess.

"I'll fill you in later," Tess replied.

"And this is Daisy." Audie continued. "She's the bison who kept going over to visit your ranch when the mean man owned it."

"I'd heard a few of your bison took a shine to wandering about," Cooper said to Audie with a teasing tone and a wide smile. The first smile Tess had seen on him tonight, as a matter of fact.

"The cat in the barn had kittens two weeks ago," Audie said to Sophie. "Wanna go see if they'll play with us?"

No little girl on the planet could say no to that request. Within seconds Sophie and Audie were racing off toward the barn, chatting and laughing as if they'd known each other for months instead of hours.

"She ratted you out, you know," Tess said as they watched the pair amble off.

Cooper merely adjusted his hat on his head and made a grunting sound.

"According to her, 'Daddy didn't want to come.' And we had a 'different of opinion.'"

Cooper put one boot up on the corral fence. "Well, I was warned."

"You were also invited. And they're having a ball, Sophie and Audie."

He looked at her. "I'm glad for that, really I am."

He didn't have to say that he wasn't sure it was worth the full-out inquisition he was putting up with tonight to give Sophie that fun. His aggravation with the questioning was clear to everyone—except, maybe, Sophie and Audie.

Tess didn't want this to be the last time

Cooper Pine set foot on the Blue Thorn Ranch. There had to be a way to bridge the gap between her family and his. "Honestly, Cooper, I don't get the secrecy. It's only hurting you, making folks suspect the worst."

She should have kept her mouth shut. Cooper's face fell sharply. "I don't owe you—any of you—more explanation than what I've said. No matter how nice you are to Sophie."

Tess pushed off the corral fence where she'd been leaning. "I would not use Sophie to get to you, ever. I'm not that kind of person, and we're not that kind of family. Sophie will always be welcome here no matter what kind of circus you decide to put on over there."

"It won't be a circus."

"Then what will it be?" Why did they always end up back at this impasse?

Cooper pushed off the fence and turned toward the barn. "Maybe we need to end this right here."

Tess put her hand out to stop him. "No, don't. I'm sorry. Let the girls have their fun."

"I'm glad *someone's* having fun this evening."

Tess forced herself to seek a way to save the evening. "Tell me about the Method. Does it work on any animal or just horses? Could you train a bison?"

He looked toward the enormous beasts. "Never tried. But it's specific to horses, not camels or cattle or bison…" He hesitated just a moment before he looked back at her and added, "Or people."

"But because of your training experience, are there things you see in animals—like Daisy and Russet here—that we can't see? Behaviors and such?" She was making an effort here. The least the man could do was to try to meet her halfway.

Cooper walked back to the portion of the fencing where Daily and Russet stood. "Can I tell that Daisy here is more comfortable around humans than the rest of your herd? Well, I expect even you can see that."

"Well, sure." Tess reached out and stroked the soft brown fur of Daisy's enormous head. It never ceased to amaze her how soft the fur was, or how sweet it smelled despite the animal's size and time in the pasture. "Here, feel her."

She watched Cooper reach out and touch the bison. It was always fun to watch people interact with Daisy. "She is soft. And huge. Must be at least a thousand pounds of animal in there. How'd she get so acclimated to people?"

"Gunner got her when her mother was killed in an accident. He was with her constantly in those first few days. She was almost newborn, so she bonded with him instead of her mother. I won't say she's a pet, but she's comfortable around us. It helps to have an animal we can show visitors up close."

"She's a fine specimen. I can tell Gunner cares a lot about his herd." Daisy gave a great snort and thrust her big black nose up against the fence, making Cooper laugh. "And the lady recognizes a compliment."

Tess offered a small smile. "All women do. Even Sophie. I think she's amazing."

Cooper looked over to the barn where the girls were surely immersed in a kitten lovefest. "She is, at that. Some days I feel like I'd offer up a leg of my own if it'd help ease the way for her, you know?"

Maybe it was talking about Daisy's lost mother, but Tess found herself asking, "Tell me about Sophie's mom."

Cooper's whole body changed at the request, his shoulders losing their defensive stance, his eyes casting back into memory. "Ah, Grace. That's where Sophie gets her amazing. Gone three years now and not a day goes by that I don't think of her." He put his hands up against the fence, brushing against the top of Daisy's head, as if touching the mama bison offered up some kind of connection to the mother of his daughter. "She didn't make it through the accident that took Sophie's leg. Gone before she made it to the hospital, before I could see her or say goodbye."

"I'm so sorry." To have someone taken from you so quickly like that? Leaving so much sadness in their wake? Tess found herself wondering if she'd even survive such a blow. She was rocking after something much less, after all. Cooper Pine must be a strong soul to have kept going like he had and to have raised Sophie, as a single dad, to be so full of joy despite her circumstances.

"After the accident," Cooper went on, "there was so much awfulness everywhere I could hardly breathe. Grace gone. Sophie so small and in so many surgeries. Police reports, funeral and such. I count it a blessing Sophie doesn't remember most of it. She couldn't even attend her own mama's funeral. Black, hard day that was. Just a giant wall of pain and sorrow."

He swallowed hard at that, and Tess felt tears tighten her own throat at his obvious pain. "That's awful. Was the accident far from home?"

Cooper nodded. "Two miles from our house. If I had been home, I probably would have heard the crash. Come running. Maybe been there for Grace's last moments."

He paused for a moment, pulling himself together, making Tess wince from the sense of asking too painful a question. "I can't even begin to imagine."

"No," he said without judgment, "you can't—no one can. The bloke in front of her had some kind of seizure, lost control of his car, spun around and T-boned Sophie and Grace at fifty miles an hour. Grace lost her life. Sophie lost her leg. I felt like I'd lost everything. Spun out of control myself for a few weeks, but I couldn't stay in a funk—Sophie needed her daddy."

"How'd you make it?"

Cooper looked at her. "Hunter. He's the only reason. I mean, Grace's folks were wonderful, but they were drowning in their own grief. My parents have been gone awhile, so it really was all Hunter. He dragged me back into life before I was ready, before I even wanted to try to face my responsibilities. Physically came over and hauled me out of bed some mornings, driving me to the hospital. He made me keep going. He kept saying 'Fake it till you feel it,' and it worked. I wasn't kidding when I said I owe a lot of who I am and what I've got to him."

"Family can pull you out of a dark place." She shouldn't have said that. Too much of her own dark place showed up in how she said the words.

He noticed. "Is that why you're home? You need pulling out of a dark place?"

She shook her head. "Nothing like yours. I'm just…having trouble figuring out what's next."

"You know," he said, straightening as if to physically pull himself out of the memory, "loads of people go through life without ever needing to know what's next. They just wait for 'next' to show up. For themselves… or their neighbors." He made his point, but he did it with more of a smile in his eyes this time.

Tess sighed as she looked into Daisy's huge brown eyes. "You know, I've just never been one of those people who can wait and see what will happen. It's a Buckton thing."

"Like to have it all mapped out, do you?"

"Let's just say I feel better at least knowing the general direction. Gunner, he's more of a specifics kind of guy. Luke is the full-speed-ahead, take-no-prisoners one of the bunch, like Gran. Nobody dares to cross Gran. Only Ellie comes close to making it up as she goes along."

"And all those Bucktons want to know what I'm up to."

"Well, some more than others." Given what she had just heard, she was inclined to trust Cooper a bit more with the privacy of his future plans, but she was sure Gunner wouldn't see it that way.

Cooper turned to face her. "I'll make you a deal, Tess Buckton. When I'm ready, you'll know." He held out his hand.

She took it, but the gesture had more to it than a simple handshake. "Deal."

He didn't let go of her hand but held it firm as he held her gaze. "Just in case you were wondering, I'm not ready." His tone was unshakable, making it clear this was a battle the Bucktons would not win. At least, not today.

She realized, feeling his firm grip on her hand, that she'd have to trust his character on this. And she'd spent the last two months paying for misjudging a man on his character. Tonight's supper was supposed to make things better, but Tess couldn't say they hadn't made things worse. She was coming to genuinely like the man who could throw the Blue

Thorn Ranch under—or maybe just right next to—a very Piney bus.

"Can I? Can I? Can-I-can-I-can-I?"

Cooper was just congratulating himself on making it through the brownies and ice cream dessert at the Buckton barbecue when Audie and Sophie came loping up to the table with a basket.

A basket that *meowed*.

"Can you have a brownie? Absolutely. You already know how good Mrs. Buckton's brownies are."

"Not that." Sophie rolled her eyes as she deposited the basket on Cooper's lap and settled herself at a table where Audie had already placed a pair of brownies and was scooping out large portions of ice cream.

"Audie..." Audie's mother Brooke said with the "what have you done?" tone every mother knows how to wield.

"We've got four, Mom. Gunnerdad said we don't need them all."

Every adult on the lawn knew what was in the works, but Cooper decided to play dumb. "What's in the basket, sunshine?" Of course, he could see—and hear—exactly what was in the basket and where Sophie believed said basket was headed: home with them.

"It's a kitten, Daddy."

Cooper feigned surprise as he looked down, gaining a Seriously? look from Tess. "So it is. Why'd you bring the kitten to dessert?"

"Audie said I could keep it."

"That's something you have to ask an adult before you make that kind of offer, Audie." Brooke turned to Cooper. "I'm so sorry about this."

"I already named it and everything," Sophie said, as if that should seal the deal.

"And what did you name this kitten that I have not yet said you could keep?" It was a tiny chance to hope that he could get out of there tonight with just naming rights, but one look at Sophie's eyes told him just how tiny that chance was. Sophie'd been wanting a pet for ages, but their lives never could accommodate even a goldfish. Now that they were at a stable location, he had been thinking about it—for later.

"Rainbow Sparkle."

Gunner practically pulled a spit-take with his iced tea, and the rest of the family burst into laughter. Tess's eyes went wide and she covered her mouth with her hands. The grandmother waved her hands in the air and guffawed.

"Better name for a kitten than a bison calf,

Gunner," Luke called out. "Didn't you say you'd never have an animal on the ranch with that name?"

"I never said that." Gunner frowned.

"Yes, you did," Audie declared.

Cooper had to admit, Audie and Sophie really did have a lot in common in addition to being wise beyond their years. Crafty beyond their years, more like it.

"Well played, young lady, well played." Luke winked at Sophie.

A kitten? thought Cooper. "I'm really more of a dog man myself." As last-ditch defenses go, it wasn't much of a winner.

"I get the feeling that won't matter too much at the moment," said Ellie's husband, Nash—who seemed like a nice bloke worth getting to know, even if he was married to a Buckton. For a guy who was the county sheriff, he'd been one of the only people not subjecting Cooper to an interrogation tonight.

"I'm sorry," Tess said, looking not the least bit sorry.

"No, you're not. Not laughing like that, you're not." He couldn't blame her, he was nearly laughing himself and he was about to gain a spontaneous pet.

"Okay, well then, I'll just say I didn't see this coming," Tess replied.

Every eye in the group stared at him, waiting for his surrender to the assault of cuteness about to descend on his household. He held up his hands. "I know when I'm beat. You can keep the little fella."

"She's a girl!" Sophie squealed as she flung herself at Cooper. He could live to be a hundred and never tire of the feeling of Sophie's arms wrapping around his neck. She was his treasure, his energy, his center, and he could never deny her anything, much less a kitten.

Sophie reached into the basket and held the little critter up, cuddling her next to her cheek in about the cutest little tableau anyone could imagine. "See how cute she is? How much she loves us already?"

Cooper had visions of his couch being "loved" into ribbons. He threw a glance Glenno's way as if to say, "Are you ready for this?" Glenno, who could likely take a typhoon in stride, simply smiled. Cooper could practically hear the man saying that Sophie needed a summer project, why not this?

"Only I'll just stick to calling her Sparkle if it's okay with you. Rainbow Sparkle's a bit much for a man of my nature."

"So I can keep her?" asked Sophie, clutching the little fur ball even tighter. His daughter either wanted extra assurances or just lots of witnesses—he couldn't decide which.

"Yes, if the Bucktons are offering her as a gift, then we accept." It bugged him to feel in the least bit indebted to this family, but this was for Sophie. Maybe, if he was fortunate, it would serve as a distraction to all the ranch business.

"You'll have to keep her here for another week or so," Brooke explained, resulting in a moan and a frown from Sophie. "She's just a bit too little to be gone from her mama just yet. But that will give you time to get her food and a collar and such."

"A rainbow collar, right?" Audie suggested. Cooper wondered if he could stomach a walk down the kitty collar aisle of any pet store in search of rainbow motifs. Maybe Brooke or Tess would chaperone that trip.

Gunner's still chilly reception warmed just a bit. "Better you than me, Pine."

Being a Pine clearly earned him no special privileges on this ranch. Quite the opposite, if he had to guess. Instead of being annoyed, Cooper rather liked it. Even if his reception felt more like "chill" than "celebrity," it at least felt authentic. No layers of optics or marketing. With all the cunning and positioning and secrecy his life had required of late, it was a welcome change. Sort of.

Ellie brought out a blanket and Audie, Sophie and Rainbow Sparkle spent the rest of dessert sprawled on it, playing and cooing.

"They're adorable," Tess offered as she scooped up the last of her ice cream.

"Off the cuteness charts, I'll grant you that." He looked at her. "I've only had puppies. Is this little critter going to keep me up nights?"

"Not if she sleeps with Sophie."

"Oh, she's sleeping with Sophie, all right. I can't have it get out that Cooper Pine sleeps with a kitty now, can I?"

"The Pine Brothers are far too rugged for kitties," she agreed. Then she narrowed one eye at him out of nowhere. "Is that why no one knows you're a dad?"

"Authentic" had just skidded over into "blunt."

"You don't hold back on anything, do you?"

"I just wondered, that's all. I was really surprised to learn you had a daughter. Surely you've made the choice to keep her out of the picture. Why?"

Wasn't it obvious? "My private life is my private life. Sophie's not a marketing tool.

The last thing she needs is an audience of people saying 'Poor Sophie.'"

"What about a bunch of people saying 'Hooray for Sophie'?"

Luke, of all people, stepped in to Cooper's defense. "You don't get one without the other, Tess. When people root for you, they feel like they own you." He ought to know what he was talking about—the man had tanked his rodeo career on live television and then fallen just short of resurrecting it in much the same way. That meant he'd seen the darker side of publicity just as Cooper had. "But I think I could strike a balance. You know, have a family but not completely hide my kids from the spotlight."

Was that a barb at Sophie's distance from the Pine Method? Cooper felt his hackles rise, but this was no place to pick a fight over something as personal as how a man handles his children—children that Luke didn't even have yet. Cooper glanced at his watch, glad to see it was close enough to Sophie's bedtime to allow a hope of a graceful exit.

"Sophie, honey, time to get ready to go. Ten more minutes with the kitten."

The expected moans of "Can't we stay longer" didn't sway him. He'd spent enough time in the public eye to know that it was best to say goodbye well before he reached the end of his patience, and it had been a demanding night. Kitten acquisition included.

Ten minutes later he finally extracted a yawning Sophie from Sparkle and Audie, and deposited her into the car. He wasn't surprised when Tess followed him.

"I'm glad you came," she offered. "It wasn't that bad, was it? I mean, you got a kitten out of the deal," she said with an apologetic smile.

"Yeah, about that…" he started to say something about Trojan horses coming in kitten form, but then he remembered that the whole point of tonight—for him at least—was to gain Sophie a friend, which she had. *Be thankful for that*, he told himself. "Thanks."

"I'll help with settling her in, if you like. And I can give free braiding lessons if you need them."

The idea of seeing Tess again made him nervous but not enough to decline. "Sure."

Her smile tugged at a part of him he didn't yet trust. "See you soon, then. Kitty in tow."

"Right then. G'night."

"Good night!" Sophie called with a sleepy wave from the back seat.

"Good night, sweetheart. See you again soon."

He liked the sound of that. And that could be a problem.

# Chapter Six

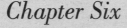

"And that's when we talked about the name and the babies and the horses." Sophie had been talking a mile a minute since she'd bounced out of bed Sunday morning.

Adele Buckton—Tess's grandmother— had, of course, invited Cooper and Sophie to attend the church in town this morning, but he'd declined. He wasn't opposed to church— not by a long shot—but he'd had his fill of Bucktons for the moment, knowing the kitty acquisition and the budding friendship with Audie would likely bring more interaction between their families.

Sophie went on, relating every detail of the evening as if he and Glenno hadn't been there. To hear her talk, it had been the high-light of her little life.

"I took you there for bison burgers and I

came home with a kitten. How did that happen?" He tried to hold his scowl but the glee in Sophie's eyes made it impossible.

She giggled. "It was a 's'posed to be,' Daddy. Audie said Rainbow Sparkle was just waiting for us to come take her home. Audie and I talked about lots of stuff."

Cooper could just imagine. "Like what?" he asked as he sat next to Sophie at the kitchen counter. The aroma of Glenno's cheesy scrambled eggs filled the kitchen. Sophie and Audie had become instant friends, and that was certainly an answer to a prayer, even if it did bring a lot of complications at the moment.

"Audie's daddy went to heaven when she was little, just like Mama."

Cooper heard Glenno's spatula still for a second and his own heart hitched at her statement. He'd heard Tess refer to her brother Gunner as Audie's stepdad, but hadn't realized Brooke had been a widow before she'd married Gunner. Young as he was, he didn't know too many people who'd been through what he'd been through with the loss of a spouse, and he tucked the information away.

"When Audie's mom married Mr. Gunnerdad, Audie got to be a flower girl at the wedding."

Cooper had heard Audie refer to her stepdad by the amusing nickname, but he hadn't expected Sophie to pick up on it. Still, "Mr. Gunnerdad" sounded too cute for him to correct her. "She did, did she?"

"She got to wear an extra-special dress and walk down the aisle of the church with her mama. She showed me a picture."

He wasn't quite sure where this was heading. "That sounds nice."

Sophie looked up at him. "Can I be a flower girl when you find a Gunnermom for me?"

Glenno coughed. Cooper swallowed hard. How to tackle the six different issues in that question? He started with the easiest. "There's no such thing as a Gunnermom. Gunnerdad is Audie's special name for her stepfather. If you ever get a stepmother, you'll get to pick your own name for her." A part of him wondered why he'd said "if." He was twenty-nine—still young enough to easily marry again.

Sophie pressed the subject further. "I get to walk down the aisle and be a flower girl, don't I?"

Glenno moved the skillet off the heat and turned to watch how Cooper was going to field this question.

The topic of his remarriage was bound to come up someday, he'd just counted on it coming a little later than this morning over breakfast. He pulled his hand across his chin. "Well, now, I haven't given it much thought, but I think you'd make a perfect flower girl." He looked into Sophie's eyes. "Have you been thinking a lot about Mama lately?"

"Audie likes having a new daddy. It made me wonder if I could like having a new mama. And being a flower girl. That sounds fun."

He thought he ought to say it. "Getting a new stepmom someday doesn't mean we love Mama in heaven any less. She'll always be your mama."

"I know."

"But getting a new stepmom is a big thing. We both have to be ready, and it has to be a very special lady."

"Super special," Sophie agreed. Then, as carefully as a six-year-old says anything, she added, "I think Miss Tess is nice, don't you?"

Glenno, after giving Cooper a look, chuckled and went back to his cooking as if to say "You're on your own with this one."

His instinct was to shut down this conversation in whatever way would be fastest—but for all that, he wasn't going to lie to his daughter and claim that he didn't like Tess at all. Tess had done him the honor of asking about Grace. Despite the tender subject, talking to Tess about Grace had felt good, comfortable—the most comfortable part of the evening, if he were honest. So, yes, he thought she was nice. Nosy, but nice. But surely that wasn't enough to get Sophie thinking about weddings. He certainly wasn't looking for romance with Tess. Not after his mess with Lynette, and certainly not with all the complications between him and the Buckton family.

"Miss Tess will be a nice friend to have," he said casually. "Who doesn't like somebody who brings you brownies on your birthday?"

Sophie laughed. "And now she'll bring Rainbow Sparkle over for visits until she's ready to come home to stay. That's nice."

Cooper realized he needed to be careful about how he talked about the pretty tawny-haired woman in front of his daughter. Wanting the frills of being a flower girl didn't necessitate the emotional drama of considering remarriage. Lynette had shown him he didn't want to try dating again for a long time.

He attempted a second change of subject. "Where will this kitty sleep? I don't want her sleeping with me. Do you want her to sleep with you, Glenno?"

"No, sir, I don't," Glenno said emphatically.

"Where on earth can a soft little kitten

sleep in this house? The barn? The garden shed? Here in the kitchen?"

"Daddy," Sophie moaned, "Rainbow Sparkle's gonna sleep with me in my room."

"You don't want a fuzzy, cute little kitty like that sleeping with you, do you?"

She realized his jest and dissolved into the giggles that were Cooper's favorite sound in the whole world.

"Yes, I do. I do!"

"In your bed? With you? She'll take up so much room. She probably snores."

"Kitties don't snore," Sophie said, still laughing. "Only Glennos snore. And she's tiny, Daddy, you saw her. She'll just go 'meow.'" With that, Sophie began offering her best kitty imitation.

Glenno slid a small plate of eggs in front of Sophie. "Glennos snore proudly," the man said, making a dramatic snoring sound right up against her ear. "We snore as good as we cook."

"And Glenno cooks very well, doesn't he, Sophie?"

Sophie nodded enthusiastically around a mouthful of cheesy eggs.

"I have a bunch of boring jobs to do this afternoon. What do you say we go for a ride right after breakfast? You did so well on Hope last time, I'd like to see you do it again."

"Sure!" Sophie agreed almost instantly.

Cooper made sure his words sounded as casual as possible as he asked, "With or without your leg?" Sophie had a decent prosthetic leg, but rarely opted to wear it. Cooper rather admired that she seemed to feel complete without it, and truth be told, she was faster on her crutches than with the device. One of the equine therapists had told her she might have an easier time riding with the leg, but so far Sophie hadn't been interested. The extra work of riding with a missing leg seemed like no problem to her. She could only do so much that way, however. While part of him wanted her to be a skilled horsewoman, another part of him was just fine letting her set the pace. She had years to learn to ride well, to grow up, to want or need to look or walk like everyone else. He adored her just the way she was, and prayed every night that he showed her so.

"Nope," Sophie said, scooping up more eggs. "Just me."

Cooper had always liked how she phrased it—it wasn't "without my leg," it was "just me." It made him feel she might really think of herself as whole without it. It had been years since his life felt whole; it was God's gift to him that his daughter felt that way about herself.

"Okay, then, a ride after breakfast it is." He poked her nose. "Just us."

The glow of a light spilled gently out from under Gran's door Sunday night, despite the late hour. "The longer you live, the less you sleep," Gran used to say, for she'd rarely boasted a decent night's rest even before Tess had left on her travels. Gran always said it was God allowing her to be up praying while the rest of the world slept, but Tess didn't really buy that sweetened explanation of this symptom of Gran's advancing age.

She swallowed hard and knocked softly. "Gran?"

"Come on in." She didn't look entirely surprised to see Tess. "Hello, hon. Still on Down Under time?"

For a split second Tess considered taking the out her grandmother just gave her and using that to explain her sleeplessness. But excuses wouldn't solve anything. There was only one solution she could see to her problems right now, and as much as she hated it, Gran was it.

"Not really," she said, coming to sit on the ottoman by Gran's upholstered wing-backed chair. According to Gran, she spent as many nights dozing in this chair as she did sleeping in bed.

The forwarded envelopes she'd picked up at the Martins Gap post office Friday were filled with overdue bills. She needed to take action or she'd be facing serious legal consequences. There was no sense in beating around the bush. "I'm in trouble, Gran."

Gran took her hand. "It isn't hard to see that."

Tess wrapped her hands around Gran's pale, small fingers. "I made a big mistake in Australia. A really big, really stupid, mistake."

Gran closed her eyes for a moment. "Bucktons are no strangers to mistakes. True of most folks, when you think of it." She held Tess's eyes. "Are you hurt?"

Now there was a question. *My heart's in a billion pieces and I feel like I can never hold my head up again.* "Not in the way you mean."

Tess waited for Gran to ask the dozen questions she knew must be buzzing around the old woman's head. "And I'm not in danger," she felt compelled to add when Gran didn't speak. "Well, not the physical kind, I mean. Trouble, yes. Danger, not really." She'd signed a six-month lease on a new, larger apartment, with a second bedroom for Bardo, on the advice of Jasper Garvey. Jasper had praised her decisive decision-making, guided her, and even wooed her off her feet—all with what she now realized was malicious intent. Very expensive malicious intent.

The last-minute change to her airfare had cost a fortune. She'd sold her car and all of her furniture to make some of the bills, and had maxed out every credit card she had to scrounge up the cash Jasper had claimed he needed for the "unofficial adoption donations" he said were part of the process. There was nothing left. Not even her pride.

Looking into Gran's eyes—eyes that had witnessed more than one life bottom out and then return to success—Tess could almost spit it out. *I used to be a smart person. You raised me to be someone who'd never make a dumb move like this. I should have done my research. I should have made inquiries. I shouldn't have trusted what Jasper told me, how he flattered me, or the people he set up for me.* All that came out was, "I've made a mess and I'm ashamed." The tears started falling with that last, piercing word.

She still wasn't ready to tell the story, but the bills wouldn't wait until she was. Gran was the most compassionate person Tess knew, but the only thing making this whole business more humiliating was having to ask Gran for help.

Her grandmother seemed to know this, for her next words were so quiet and tender. "What do you need?"

The word she needed to say wrapped around her throat like a noose. Tess took as big a breath as she could manage given the steel bands of guilt squeezing her lungs and forced it out. "Money."

Gran was quiet for a moment, nodding.

"I owe people money."

That was an oversimplification, to say the least. What she'd done was an all-out foolish calamity. "I led with my heart and it all went to pieces," she wanted to say but couldn't. "Leading with her heart" sounded noble, when the truth was that she'd only been foolish and too stubborn to admit defeat until it was too late. She hadn't taken the time to find out how the Australian adoption program worked. She'd just seen Jasper as the path to happiness and to Bardo and done what he'd told her to do.

Only there were no paths to Bardo. Jasper's unconventional work-around had turned out to be a scheme to swindle a huge adoption fee. Of course, that wasn't at all "how it's done." She'd been had, pure and simple. By a man who'd romanced her with grand gestures of love, but who turned out to be a con artist. A dupe she should have been smart enough to see coming, but didn't. After all, this was the age of the internet. She could have had information at her fingertips had she just taken the time to look for it. Humiliating.

"How much money?"

More than Gran could afford to give painlessly, Tess knew that. She shut her eyes, feeling a line of tears streak down from each as she did. "Twelve thousand."

She opened her eyes in time to see the shock on Gran's face. There was at least a little validation in her grandmother's surprise. It was proof that she wasn't making a mountain out of a molehill, and now someone else knew it.

"That's a lot of money," Gran said carefully.

That was just what was left of the debt, not the entire twenty-two thousand she'd sunk into the deal. No, not the deal, the *con*. She'd been conned.

The worst part was that Bardo would have been worth it. *Bardo*. Her heart sank at the memory of his face. Was he lonely? Did he wait for her to show up and bring him home every day? Did he ask anyone at the services home why she hadn't come for him like she said she would? Her own faults were bad enough, but to know Bardo had paid a price for her foolishness, too? It stung as if someone had cut her heart out. Because, in so many ways, someone had.

"Is this a loan?" Gran asked.

"I want it to be." In truth, she felt so knocked down that any kind of comeback—emotional or financial—seemed far out of reach. A stronger woman would fight back, hire a lawyer, call in the authorities. And if such a battle could win her Bardo, she'd have waged it from the start.

But it wouldn't. It might serve justice to stop the crooks from preying on someone else. From leading someone else to believe that adopting was one of those problems that, if you just threw enough money at it, could be solved. But she couldn't summon the energy for it. She wasn't strong or noble enough right now for such a war.

She'd already lost her battle, with no hope of future wins. There were no paths to Bardo for her. The boy could never be hers, no matter how she could hear his voice saying, "Tessy," in that pleading, heartrending way he had. *It doesn't matter that he's supposed to be with me. It doesn't matter how much I need him.* All she could do was pray that some perfect Australian family would see past his malformed hand the way she saw past Sophie's missing leg and give him the love all bound up and directionless in her own heart.

She couldn't even bring herself to write him a letter, couldn't find the words to explain to him the mess she'd made of trying to become his mom. The six unfinished letters in the bottom of her suitcase held testament to that lost cause.

The tears were coming steady now and she didn't hide them from Gran. The words weren't ready, but the tears would show Gran this was a last-ditch plea where no other help was found. She wasn't one of the happy-ending Buckton siblings, but she could ask Gran to love her and help her anyway.

"It's a mess, Gran, and it's all my fault. I'm so ashamed." The final word seemed to let loose the flood of tears, and Tess crumpled to the floor to lay her head on Gran's lap and sob, the way she had as a little girl.

"Messes are where God works best, child. We hate 'em, on account of how much they hurt, but they can be powerful things." She stroked Tess's hair, just like she used to when Tess was young.

"I can't tell you what happened yet," she cried into Gran's lap.

"Are you sure? This seems an awful big burden to bear alone."

"I'm too humiliated."

Gran used her fingers to lift Tess's head to meet her gaze. "To kill a shame you must speak its name. Silence isn't your friend here, no matter what you're facing."

Some part of her knew that. But she had to be stronger before she could admit how weak and senseless she'd been.

Giving a great big sniff and reaching for one of the tissues on the side table beside Gran, Tess said, "Soon. Not yet, but soon."

Gran cupped her chin with such compassion Tess almost started crying all over again. "I'll make some calls in the morning. It won't be easy or quick."

Tess knew that. There was nothing easy or quick to be had in any of this. She knew exactly how big a favor she was asking of Gran. Just because the ranch was doing well didn't necessarily mean Gran had funds to spare. "Thank you" didn't seem nearly enough. This was a whole new debt of another kind, even deeper than the first.

# Chapter Seven

The banging of pots and pans—along with some very enticing smells—let Cooper know Glenno was experimenting in the kitchen this afternoon. Ellie's husband, Nash, had bragged to Glenno about the ribs from a place called Red Boots just outside of town, and Glenno had gone out to get some the day after the dinner at the Blue Thorn. Now, two days later, Glenno was seeking to duplicate the recipe in anticipation of the coming Memorial Day weekend. By the racket Cooper could hear from his desk, it wasn't going well.

"Keep at it, mate. By the smell of it, you're coming close," Cooper said to himself as he sat at his computer. He was working on a spreadsheet for a crucial financing meeting with the bank. They wanted detailed cost, income and asset projections for Pine Purpose

Ranch. The numbers were daunting; he'd already brought four therapy-trained horses onto the ranch, but to fulfill his plans he'd need at least four more plus several therapists to oversee sessions. This was an expensive proposition. But he couldn't keep staring at the spreadsheets forever. He needed to finish this business plan before Tess brought Audie and Rainbow Sparkle—it made him wince even to think the kitten's silly name, much less speak it aloud—over for a visit after Audie got out of school.

Something about her eagerness to visit here told him Tess didn't feel much more comfortable on the Blue Thorn than he did—only he didn't know why. It made no sense that she felt unwelcome on her own family ranch. And yet there was that bit of a lost look in her eyes, the too erect and defensive way she held her spine around her siblings. As if they all had something on her. As if she didn't measure up against the rest of them.

"Dad?"

Cooper began closing down the spreadsheet without looking up. "What, sunshine?"

"What do you think?"

Strawberry-blond curls popped up over the top of his laptop, followed by a wide set of eyes, followed by a very squiggly set...of whiskers. Sophie had drawn whiskers onto her face. "Whoa, there!" he exclaimed as he closed the lid. "Where'd you get those?"

Sophie lifted her nose as if to let him admire her handiwork. With a lack of makeup in the house, Cooper dearly hoped that wasn't permanent marker on her face. "I want Rainbow Sparkle to feel at home when she comes to visit," she said as she modeled her new accessory.

Sophie really was hungry for company. "I think she likes you as a little girl, not a cat."

At which point Sophie produced a sort of headband thing with furry cat ears he vaguely remembered from some dress-up costume. "I'm both."

He poked her on her little girl-kitty nose. "That you are, sunshine."

Sophie propped her crutches against his desk and crawled up into his lap. Purring, of course. "Well, now, it seems I'm to be expecting two kitties at my house today. I don't know that I'm ready for that."

She looked up at him with wonder-wide eyes. "You want some whiskers, too? You can be the daddy kitty."

Cooper was in no rush to greet Tess Buckton at his door sporting a set of kitty whiskers. He made a big show of scratching his unshaved chin on Sophie's forehead. "I've already got whiskers."

She giggled and rubbed her forehead. "I forgot. But you can wear my ears." She plucked the fuzzy ears from her head and stretched the small headband over Cooper's head. He was grateful it popped right off.

"I've already got ears, too. Those are for you, anyway."

"How much longer till Rainbow Sparkle gets here?"

Cooper pulled his watch into view. "What's that number there?"

Sophie squinted at the watch. "It's a three."

"And when the longer hand is on the bottom six, Miss Tess and Audie will come. That's only ten minutes. You can wait ten minutes, can't you?"

"It'll be hard. I been waiting all morning. Glenno's busy, too."

Cooper took a great big sniff. "Ah, but Glenno's busy smells delicious, don't you think?"

The gate buzzer on the intercom sounded, sending Sophie into cheers. "They're here!" She hopped over to the intercom box on the study wall, pushed the speak button and shouted "Hello!" into the speaker. She wasn't supposed to answer the intercom on her own, but he didn't have the heart to scold her when she was so excited.

"It's Tess and Audie." The scratchy voice came over the device.

"And Rainbow Sparkle," said Audie.

"We're a bit early," added Tess. "Is that okay?"

"Audie's here!" Sophie said.

Cooper, who'd risen and was standing beside Sophie handing her the crutches, hit the button. "Of course it is, come on up." He tapped the button, unlocking the gate, and followed Sophie out the door.

Moments later Tess and Audie stood on his doorstep, Rainbow Sparkle mewing from the same basket she'd arrived in at the barbecue Saturday.

"Visiting kitten service," Tess announced with a smile, nodding toward Audie. "Because *someone* couldn't stand to wait one minute longer."

Cooper peered down at the cat. "Well, Sparkle, I'd pegged you for a more patient kitty than that."

"I'm the one that couldn't wait, Mr. Pine," Audie explained with a giggle.

Sophie gave a little hop. "Neither could I."

"You've got whiskers!" Audie said.

"Want some?" Sophie asked. "We can all have 'em."

"Can I?" Audie looked up at her aunt.

"Hang on, there," Cooper interrupted. "I haven't seen which marker made those whiskers. We can't send Audie home with something that won't wash off."

"I'll go get it. Come on, Audie, I can show you my room."

With that, the girls raced off, leaving Tess, Cooper and Rainbow Sparkle standing in the front hallway until Audie raced around the corner, snatched up the basket full of kitty and sprinted off in the direction of Sophie's room.

Tess gave a curious sniff. "Glenno attempting Red Boots' ribs?"

"He is. We'd best steer clear of the kitchen while he works. Why don't we go into the big room?"

"Smells like he's getting close to me."

"I'm sure whatever he's got is delicious. I find it's pretty easy to support Glenno's hobby."

"Daddy, look!" Sophie and Audie came back into the living room, Sophie pointing to a tiny, pink-leather collar around the kitten's neck as Audie held her.

"Luke made it. A bit of an olive branch, I think."

"There's a litterbox and some kitten food in the back of the truck, too," Tess added. "We didn't know if you'd had a chance to go out and get kitten fixings yet."

"Been sort of dragging my feet on that, to be honest," he whispered, bringing him a bit too close to Tess. She smelled really good. A clean sort of floral—feminine, but not too fancy.

"Well, now you've got the basics. Brooke says about one more week, and then she's yours for good."

"What do you say, Sophie?"

"Thank you," Sophie said with a wide smile. "I love the collar. She loves it, too, don't you think?"

"What little girl doesn't like pink?" Tess offered.

"I was expecting rainbows and sparkle," Cooper joked.

"I think even Luke knew you had limits," Tess said as she reached into her pocket. "But here's my contribution." She produced a long ribbon with a ball of tin foil tied onto the end. "Homemade kitten entertainment." She dangled the toy over the tiny cat, who lunged and pawed so comically that the girls cooed in unison.

"You just bought me an hour's worth of peace and quiet, I think."

Tess grinned. "At least for now."

The girls raced off to Sophie's room, kitten, collar and toy in tow. The trail of fading giggles made Cooper smile. He had to find a way to make peace with his neighbors, for Sophie's sake if not for his own. "Tess…" he began, wiping his hands down his face. He had no idea what to say, but needed to say something. "Can we find a way out of this standoff?"

She looked after the girls. "Didn't we just do that?"

"Well, in terms of Sophie and Audie maybe."

"But not in terms of…" At first he thought she was going to say "you and I," which felt dangerous but not altogether wrong, but she said, "Bucktons and Pines."

It had to be said. "You could give me ten kittens—and please don't—but it won't change my mind about telling you my plans before I'm ready." It struck him. "That's not why you gave Sophie the kitten, is it?"

She frowned. "Haven't we been through this? No one is using that kitten to try and bribe your plans out of you."

"Well, when you put it that way, it does sound rather underhanded." Wow, he really had become jaded about people and their motivations. He offered her a seat in one of the chairs that looked out the windows framing a view of the pastures. "I just… I just didn't expect it, that's all."

"You're kind of a celebrity. I'd think people would be nice to you all the time."

"There's nice and then there's nice with an agenda."

"And you think Rainbow Sparkle comes with an agenda attached." She didn't think very highly of his interpretation, the sarcasm in her tone made that clear. He was botching this left and right.

"Well, I don't *now*."

"But you did Saturday night?"

"You want something from me I've said I'm not going to give you. I've known you one week and you gave my daughter a kitten. Wouldn't you be just a bit suspicious?"

She sat back. "I suppose I could see how you might question it. But I assure you this was much more about Audie and Sophie than you and the rest of us. How about we just take this at face value and try not to read so much into little girls and kittens?"

That certainly made more sense to him.

Of course, now that she was here, and the girls were off in kitten-cuteness mode, it struck Cooper that he'd actually have to entertain this woman for an hour or two. As host duties went, it wasn't that bad a prospect. "You said you've never seen the place. Would you like to take a walk around?" It was a nice day, not too hot and pleasantly breezy for May.

She seemed to realize he was putting forth an effort. "Yes, I'd like that."

He stood, grateful to have something to do. "We'll cut through the kitchen and let Glenno know we'll be outside."

She smiled. "I'd like to see how he's faring. Mastering Red Boots' recipe would be quite an accomplishment."

"Harder than Lolly's at least. By the way, there's a tin of Glenno's version of Lolly's blondies in the pantry. I think a woman bearing kittens and kitten-related gifts earns at least two blondies, don't you think?"

There was the return of her smile again. "Go ahead, twist my arm."

"Tess!" Glenno greeted the guest with an easy smile as he looked up from a bowl of thick red sauce. "Thank you for the meal Saturday."

"Oh, yeah, thanks," offered Cooper, feeling

awkward at his tension when Glenno seemed to welcome Tess like she was an old friend. "I forgot my manners."

"You're welcome, both of you."

"Perhaps I'll send you back with some cherry pie as a show of thanks." Glenno held out a spoon of the sauce for Tess to try. "Am I close?"

Tess tested the sauce. He expected her to laugh it off, but she looked thoughtful as she licked her lips. "Really close. Hey, the church has a picnic every fall. There's usually a baking contest. You could make a pretty good showing." She turned to Cooper. "If you're still here."

"We'll see" was all he said as he pulled off the top of the tin and offered the blondies to Tess. "We're going out for a walk, Glenno. Think you can keep the girls from disaster until we get back?"

Another wave of giggles pealed down the hallway from the direction of Sophie's bedroom. "I think I'll be fine, boss."

Blondies in hand, Tess walked through the door Cooper held open. The front room had opened onto a flagstone terrace, but the kitchen back door opened onto a freshly trimmed yard with a fence and then onto another expanse of land like the rolling hills that surrounded the ranch house.

"Will you keep the name?"

Cooper saw that for the small test that it was. "No."

Her hopes for any further explanation went unmet, so she shifted topics. "Do you miss Australia?"

Cooper gestured toward the footpath that led out through the far end of the fence. "Not too much. Hunter's here, my folks are gone, and Grace's parents stay in touch. I've got some mates there I don't see often enough, but I've got mates like that everywhere. I've been keeping too tight a schedule lately, so it makes keeping up friendships hard."

"Hard for Sophie, too? A little girl needs friends."

"It's part of why we're here."

He wasn't going to open up much more than that; she could see it in his eyes. Cooper Pine was a puzzle—gregarious and personable, but with a solid wall around him. He had broad shoulders and an athletic build, but instead of the lithe, lazy grace of her twin brother, Luke, Cooper held himself erect, almost at attention. On guard, she realized. Intentionally but almost imperceptibly aloof. She wondered if all famous—or even semi-famous—people acquired such a skill for being charming but distant.

"I think you should take Gran's suggestion about coming to church. Sophie'd make a bunch of friends there, and they have lots of great programs for kids her age." On a hunch she added, "They'd be fine about her... leg, you know, if that's what you're worried about. In about two seconds all they'd see is a sweet little girl."

He shook his head. "That doesn't always happen like you'd think. We've been places where I felt like I've had to come out and say 'there's a little girl between those crutches, you know.' It's not that the people are bad or cruel—they just don't know how to deal with anything different. And, yes, Sophie's young, but she picks up more than people realize."

"That shouldn't have to happen."

A sad, quiet sigh escaped his lips. "Lots of things in Sophie's life shouldn't have had to happen."

"I lost my mama young, too, you know. It changes you, how you see the world." Tess reached down to the tall grasses that swept around their legs and pulled a bright yellow-and-pink Indian Blanket flower up from the brush. "Gran always said 'it makes you who you are, and you've got to trust God with the wisdom of that.'"

"Your gran has a lot of faith in that wisdom."

"She's lost a lot in her life, too. She and my grandpa were one of those great love stories, you know? The ones we all hope to have but most of us never do? Mama and Dad weren't so great a story, if you know what I mean. Or rather, the story didn't have a very happy ending. They were good together, but Dad sort of fell apart when Mama died and never put himself back together." She recognized the poignancy of that remark given Cooper's history and stifled the urge to touch his shoulder and soften the rigidity she saw there.

"It did, you know," Tess went on. "Make me who I am, I mean. Not all of it's good, but I like to think some of it is." She ventured a warm look in Cooper's direction as she turned the flower between her fingers. "Sophie's beautiful. Inside and out. I'm sure you had a lot to do with that, and that it's been hard." That felt awfully personal—and it was not like her to go so deep with someone she didn't know well. Especially not after the burn she'd received in Adelaide. Still, Cooper had this "walking wounded" quality about him, a scarred-over, numbed air that tore at her in the same way that Bardo's "life will never get better" eyes had. Both of them were too young and too strong to have the wind knocked out of them so completely.

Cooper was silent for a while, walking through the wide-open landscape, but then he turned to Tess with a protective father's piercing eyes. "I guard Sophie with my life, Tess. I won't stand for her getting hurt. Not one bit."

Tess felt stung that he'd even think her capable of it. Then again, people had showed her they were capable of wounds far beyond her imagining, hadn't they? "Cooper, I'd never…"

"She hasn't got a mama." The words flashed hard and sharp in his eyes. "It kills me…it has killed me every day since the accident…but I can't change that. So she latches on to anything that feels like…" He squinted his eyes shut, and Tess glimpsed a man fighting to stay above his boiling point. "I just can't have her hurt. Not by anyone."

Seeing him right now, the righteous fury of his protectiveness, it made sense why he kept her from the spotlight, why no Pine Brothers' fans knew about Sophie. But keeping her sheltered also meant keeping her isolated from everyone since Grace's passing—she didn't need to hear any history to guess that. It might be safe, but it sure sounded lonely.

Tess pulled herself up to match Cooper's glare. "I like Sophie. Genuinely. I'm not—we're not—playing some game to use her to learn your plans. You may not think someone's word counts for much, but I—" she felt her own hesitation pinch tight around her heart "—still do and you have my word there is nothing but affection for a sweet little girl going on here."

He looked like he wanted to believe her—that was the best way to describe his expression of guarded acceptance. Tess realized that she needed him to believe her. She needed to know that what Jasper had done to her hadn't stolen her integrity along with her dignity. Her word was still her bond, even if Jasper's had been pure deceit.

"I want Sophie and Audie to be friends. I want us to be friends," she dared to add. "I hope that's possible with all this stuff between the Blue Thorn and—" she waved her hands at the space between their properties "—here."

Cooper locked his eyes on her for a long,

unsettling moment before saying, "Pine Purpose Ranch. The place will be called Pine Purpose Ranch."

"If you buy it, you mean." He'd been careful to keep that transaction in the hypothetical realm.

"*When* I buy it." There was not one shred of "if" in that man's eyes.

There was also a distinct lack of "Pine Method" in the name, which was as big a clue as he'd given to date. Everything the Pine Method did had its name all over it—wouldn't its newest chunk of property bear the Pine Method brand?

Did he realize he'd just given her what she'd asked for—a declaration that while he wouldn't release his plans, he would admit they didn't include the Pine Method franchise? Or was he that wily that he could make her think he'd given her a revelation that he hadn't actually provided?

"So you're staying, permanently." She didn't quite know how to phrase it—everything felt like it required tiptoes and positioning.

"We are."

"And you'll allow Sophie and Audie to be friends?"

"There's been a transaction involving kittens and pink things—I'm pretty sure that's irrevocable now." The tiniest bit of the showman's glint returned to his eyes.

He believed her, believed the purity of her motives. It settled something in Tess that had been out of place since long before this whole mess began. "Irrevocable kittens?"

"A mix of metaphors, I know, but I think you know what I mean."

Tess felt herself smile. "I do, actually." She raised an eyebrow at him. "You trust Audie, but you'll keep an eye on the rest of us Bucktons."

His grin admitted she'd backed him into a bit of a corner. He'd have to come out and say he was willing to trust her, not just hint at it. "Well, all the *other* Bucktons. Except maybe Gran."

She pointed at Cooper. "Oh, don't you count Grannie B out. She's cannier than she looks." Just out of sheer affection, Tess added, "Rather like your Sophie. Smart and stubborn as her father, is she?"

Cooper rolled his eyes. "More." His shoulders lost more of their hard edge. "She's needed the determination, the little munchkin. But, trust me, that stubborn streak has a dark side. Some days it's hard to win a battle against that little girl." He nodded back in the direction of the house. "As yonder kitten proves, eh?"

"Yes," she laughed, "as yonder kitten proves."

# Chapter Eight

They walked on in companionable silence for a while until Cooper asked, "What did you do in Australia? Why were you there?"

She tread carefully with her answer, wanting to stay away from the tender subject of Bardo. "I'm a photographer. A bit of a photojournalist, too, sometimes. I bounced between jobs for travel magazines and websites." Tess wondered if the past tense of that verb stuck out as much to him as it did to her. "Well," she amended, "it's probably more accurate to say I fed my travel habit by selling pictures. I'm not on staff anywhere or anything that impressive."

"Were those canyon shots I saw in the living room Saturday night yours?"

It pleased her that he'd noticed the set of framed photographs in the ranch house living room. "Yes. Those were Gunner's favorites. I had them framed for him as a wedding present when he married Brooke."

"They're beautiful."

He struck her as the kind of man who didn't use words like that very often. She shrugged, feeling uncomfortable with the compliment. With all the blows she'd taken lately, nothing about her felt very beautiful anymore.

"They're just pictures. I have lots of pretty pictures to show for my last few years, but I'm afraid not much else." Did she look as damaged as she felt? Did the constant skittish, unmoored feeling show on her face like some kind of troubled animal? She chose to shift the subject off herself. "Cooper, can I tell you something?"

He gave her a bit of a surprised look. "Sure."

She wasn't quite sure how to start this, but it felt important, and part of the reason she hadn't just dropped Audie and the kitten off. "When I was in Sophie's room the first day I visited, she showed me a bunch of dolls."

"She has lots, that's for sure."

Tess ran her hands across a fallen tree trunk they had passed and then sat on it. "She said something that's stuck with me ever since."

Cooper sat, as well. "Which was…?"

"She said, 'Of course, none of them look like me.'"

She could see him absorb the weight of that. The statement hit him the way it hit her. "We were talking about those dolls you can buy with the hair and eyes that match a girl's," she went on. "Audie has one I got her for her first birthday as part of our family. The company is from Canada and I ran into the marketing VP on an airplane once. I forget how I mentioned it, but Sophie knew what I was talking about." Tess looked right up at Cooper. "She wasn't talking about how none of the doll's hair and eyes look like hers."

Cooper looked out over the landscape. "A year or so ago I was playing paper dolls with her." He laughed softly. "Yeah, I know, hard to picture, but a friend had sent a set of Texas cowgirl ones, so how could I say no?"

Tess smiled. "You're right. I can't quite picture you playing paper dolls."

"Well, I stuck to the manly art of cutting clothes out while she stuck them on the people. Then she held up one doll with curly hair and asked me to snip off the leg so it looked like her."

Tess sucked in her breath.

"Went through me like a knife, I tell you. Only she wasn't sad or angry or heartbroken like I was, it was just a calm kind of fact for her." He ran his hand across the back of his neck. "I choked up as I cut that paper doll. I wanted to run from the room. I couldn't speak for half an hour, maybe more. Sophie, she just got what she needed and went right on playing. That's Sophie's whole life, and Sophie's whole strength, all wrapped up in that one moment right there."

Tess felt tears prick her eyes. "She's so special, Cooper. Surely you know that."

He nodded. "I can still see that paper leg flutter to the floor while I struggled to find the right thing to say. Grace would have known a better way to handle it."

Tess knew, at that moment, that she'd done the right thing by bringing the painful subject up. Here was one tiny problem in Sophie's life she could actually fix, do one sliver of good to counter all the useless mistakes of Adelaide. "I remembered something that Canadian marketing woman said to me, and I went and looked it up last night. They have a division that alters the dolls to look like kids with disabilities. They really can make a doll that looks just like Sophie. A charity pays for the cost of manufacturing the doll and the shipping it from Canada." She put her hand on Gunner's arm. "Please, please let me ask for one for Sophie. I know it's a big gesture and we don't know each other well, but all I can tell you is I just have to do this. Please let me."

Cooper looked at her, shock and gratitude and pain all sweeping across his features. "You'd do that?" he choked out when he could finally speak. It was the first time she truly saw the man's armor drop, and she felt the muscles in his arm work under her hand.

"I'd love to. I don't know why she told me, but I'm glad she did. I feel like I've lost my ability to make a difference in the world. Let me make this difference for Sophie. It's not a ploy, I promise. I just really need to make her happy."

He stared at her in disbelief for a moment, then shook his head. He looked down, and she could tell he'd been genuinely touched by her offer. "Yes, you can get it for her. Thank you." Then, after he gained a bit more composure, he laughed. "She'll go nuts when it arrives, you know that."

"I'm planning on Sophie going nuts," Tess said. He was still a bit stunned she'd made such an offer, not really knowing what to say. "I'll have it rush-shipped to Blue Thorn so I can bring it by personally," she went on. There was a warmth, an unsettling charge in the air between them, and he searched for a way to get past it.

"So you think Sophie can be happy here?" he said, standing up to continue their walk.

"Absolutely," she replied, rising with him.

"You have lots of happy memories of your childhood here, then?"

"I had a good childhood, considering." It didn't take a trainer's instincts to see the tension that flashed over her features before she'd answered.

Cooper adjusted his hat as he walked. "That sounds like a mighty big 'considering,' if you ask me. And from the way you talked about your work, it sounds like you've been away for a while. What brought you back?"

She paused a telling moment before shrugging and saying, "It was time to come home."

"If you don't mind my saying, you spend an awful lot of time getting off the Blue Thorn for a person who claims it was time to come home."

Tess looked off in the direction of the Blue Thorn. "They're all so…happy."

Well, that spoke volumes. "And you're not." When she didn't refute it, he ventured, "Do they know? That you're not happy, I mean."

Her sigh seemed to pull the strength right out of her body. "Gran knows something's wrong, just not what, exactly. Everybody else suspects, I suppose."

"So the relentless Buckton inquisition is only for neighbors, not one of their own?" Cooper realized the harshness of that insinuation and backpedaled, leaning up against the fence they walked beside. "Sorry. That came out a bit sharper than I'd like."

She leaned up beside him against the fence, so that they stared off over the land together. "I deserved it." It was the closest she'd come to him physically, and he felt her presence buzz in the air between their shoulders. An unwelcome awareness woke up in him, the potent difference between "people" nearby and "a woman" close by.

Tess could frustrate him with a handful of words and still pull his heart up into his throat with the tender way she looked at Sophie. It made him worry—and wonder—what one tender look his way would do. That wasn't a place he should allow himself to go, at least not yet, not with everything unsettled the way it was.

He tried a trainer tactic. "What are you feeling?"

She startled off the fence at the question, making Cooper realize that, outside of horse training, the question took on unintended tones. "It's a question I ask clients," he explained. "Whatever emotions an owner displays gets picked up by the horse. So don't tell me the details—unless you want to, of course—just tell me the dominant emotion you're feeling right now."

"Why?"

He actually didn't have an answer for that. He stuffed his hands into his pockets and admitted, "Because I'm not them." Half of him really wanted to know what was putting that look in her eyes, while the other half of him shunned the idea of getting closer to her with a question like that.

She was silent for a moment and he could see her deciding how honest to be. Many times in answer to that question clients would tell him what they thought he wanted to hear, which only led to more prodding to get at the honest answer. He was grateful Tess was making the effort at honesty, even though he could see how difficult it was for her.

Tess put her hands on the top rail of the fence, as if the wood would help hold her up. She looked out across the field then lowered her eyes to the ground in front of her feet. "Shame."

She'd said it quietly, but he felt it hit him like a gust of wind. Lots of emotions were involved with the owners of problem horses, but rarely this one. She seemed to almost shrink at the utterance and, without thinking, he put his hand on her shoulder.

And then realized what he'd done. And it wasn't just his head that realized he'd touched her, his whole body took notice of the contact.

"I'm ashamed." She spit the words out, but in more resignation than anger. Still, she didn't meet his eyes but kept looking at the ground and tightened her grip on the fence rail. Her body language was closed off and yet she didn't shrug her shoulder away from his touch. He gave himself permission to keep his hand where it was.

She'd had the wind knocked out of her and was trying to find a way to stand back up. Nothing in his trainer skills applied to this but, personally, he knew what it was like to be knocked flat by life. "Thank you," he said as gently as he could.

That drew her gaze up. "For what?" The threat of tears glistened in her eyes, tucked behind that emotional shield he'd seen her raise more than once.

"For trusting me with that. It's no small thing."

Tess leaned against the fence. "You're telling me."

He moved his hand from her shoulder, leaning instead right next to her on the fence. "So why'd you do it? Whatever it was—and I really don't need to know—what emotion drove you to do whatever it is you did?" People made wrong choices when it came to the animals in their care for any number of reasons. Pride, pity, wanting to be someone they weren't, impulsiveness—the list went on as long as the episodes of Pine Method shows and longer.

"Love. I think. It came out of nowhere and it was so strong." She laughed, but sourly. "I thought I'd met my destiny, if you can believe that." Her waves of tawny hair tossed as she shook her head. "I was wrong. Hugely, stupidly, wrong." She paused for a moment before she added, "Only I wasn't. I mean, I still feel that love. But I can't do anything with it. And I'm left holding the whole mess of it having accomplished nothing." The last word held a host of bitterness. "Can we not talk about it?"

"Sure. I didn't mean to pry." Except that he did. He wanted to know what had done this to her. What mistake—in the name of love, no less—had reduced her to walking around with such wounds? He recognized the state of "the walking wounded" as Hunter called it. That thin shell of functionality a soul pastes over giant, gaping pain just so you can get through the day and stop all those kindly probing questions. He'd been the walking wounded for years after Grace died—it wasn't hard to spot the signs.

He'd always been drawn to hurting people—and the world of horse training was filled with people projecting their own problems onto animals—but this was taking on far too personal a tone for him. The hole in his chest, the one wide-open since Grace's passing, had started to demand his attention. The numbness that had swallowed the pain was giving way to something he barely recognized as loneliness. Incompleteness. That had to be coming from the fact he was about to jettison his business partner, yes? That he was standing on the brink of alienating Hunter by pulling out of the show for the crazy dream of opening an equine therapy ranch?

"We'd best get back," he said, he words stiff and uncomfortable. "Those girls could be up to anything with that kitten."

"You're right," she agreed quickly, starting to walk back toward the kitchen even before he pushed off the fence.

# Chapter Nine

*Sophie doesn't care. Sophie's glad to be here. Don't teach her to be afraid.* Cooper kept repeating that to himself as he opened the SUV door Sunday morning and saw the splendid sight of his daughter dressed up for church. In neat, even pigtails, to boot. He'd daydreamed about taking his daughter to a church—a church they could call "their" church—for months. Everything he was doing now was to be part of a community, to be making a life instead of keeping a schedule. But that didn't stop it from scaring him to death.

Gran and Tess's suggestion was a fine idea until Cooper realized it would be introducing Sophie to a whole bunch of strangers all at once. He'd actually considered suggesting to Sophie that she wear her prosthetic leg—and that bothered him immensely. He was a coward for not wanting her to stand out today because he was afraid of the reaction she'd generate. He was ashamed that he'd spent even a moment strategizing that she stood out less when she used the prosthetic, especially in a longer skirt and boots like she was wearing.

He wanted to end the constant internal war to protect her from stares and awkward questions, and the overblown welcomes folks gave a child with a disability. He cringed on Sophie's behalf when people tried *so hard*. But at least they tried, and the truth was that only *he* took things so personally, never Sophie.

"Hi, Sophie!" Audie came running up to Sophie while they were still in the church parking lot. There they were, the whole crowd of Bucktons, walking into church in a flurry of waves and "Good mornings!"

The girls hugged, Audie once again admiring Sophie's gleaming white cowboy boot. He felt a tiny surge of pride when Audie complimented Sophie's pigtails, and Tess gave him a discreet thumbs-up.

"Dad, can I sit with Audie?"

Cooper's heart froze. He'd wanted to keep Sophie by his side for this first encounter. "Um, how about *we* sit with Audie?"

"Sure. That way I can sit with Audie and

you can sit with Miss Tess. She's right over there with Audie's mom."

That wasn't why he'd suggested it, but the dreamy-eyed look in Sophie's eyes told him that was how she took it. Before he could say anything, Sophie headed on over toward them with a loud pronouncement. "We're gonna sit with you, okay?"

Well, there were worse things to endure than sitting through Sunday services with a pretty lady by his side, and the sight of Tess all done up in a stunning blue sundress was certainly no pain to behold. A woman's look hadn't caught his eye like that in a long time. When she smiled and gushed over Sophie's pigtails, Cooper felt it tighten his gut.

They walked toward the church entrance, Tess's family offering pleasant hellos even if Luke did still shoot him a sideways glance as the men removed their hats to go inside. He noted, with gratitude, that Tess led all the Bucktons up the ramp built in beside the church steps so that Sophie could join them.

"Well, hello, there, young lady," the pastor said in welcome as Sophie approached. "I haven't met you yet."

"G'day, Pastor." Cooper extended a hand. "I'm Cooper Pine and this is my daughter, Sophie."

The pastor offered a firm shake. "Is that

right? I'd heard you were in town. I'm Theo Kennedy. Delighted to see you and Miss Sophie here this morning." He glanced down at Sophie. "Any friend of Audie's is a friend of mine, Sophie. We're glad you're here."

"Thanks." Sophie beamed.

The Bucktons—everyone except Nash and Ellie who was home on bed rest about to give birth to twins—filled up a whole pew when combined with Cooper and Sophie. Sophie nearly ordered Tess to sit next to Cooper while Audie's parents, Brooke and Gunner, flanked their very fidgety toddler, Trey, followed by Grandmother Adele and Luke and his fiancée, Ruby, on one aisle. Audie insisted she and Sophie sit on the far end so they could go up to the children's message. "I'm older than that," Audie said with great ceremony, "but I wouldn't want to go up alone my first time."

Sophie shrugged. "Daddy says there isn't a shy bone in my body."

"I don't doubt it," Tess said, smiling.

"We get to church some," Cooper admitted in a low whisper. "But it'd be nice to have a true church home again."

Tess offered him an understanding look. "Everybody should have a church home, a place where they belong." She looked up into the broad beams that curved into arched rafters. "I've missed this place."

The church service was warm and simple; good teaching, hearty singing, the requisite announcements about committees and potlucks Cooper had seen everywhere. Still, he spent a good deal of time being amazed at the company he currently kept. Calling things cordial between him and the Bucktons was putting a shine on it, definitely. He'd expected a bit of bristling as he'd sat with the Bucktons, but short of a few surprised looks, no one seemed to care.

He was beginning to feel like the whole church experiment wouldn't be as bad as he'd feared, until it came time for the children's message. Audie and Sophie wandered down the aisle to sit with the other younger congregants in a circle around Pastor Kennedy.

"Audie," began the pastor, "why don't you introduce your new friend?"

"This is Sophie. She lives across the road from me."

One little boy stared at Sophie, his gaze bouncing between Sophie's crutches and the hem of her skirt. Cooper felt his stomach twist, and he saw Tess's hand go up to her mouth.

"You've only got one leg," the little boy

said, pointing, launching his mother into a run from her pew to shush the boy while gasps of shock echoed in the pews.

Tess started to rise herself, but Cooper put out a hand to stop her. He dearly wanted to save Sophie from this, but he also knew his rushing up now would only make things worse.

"That's right," said Sophie, astoundingly unfazed. "How many you got?"

"Everybody's got two," the boy said, earning him a harsh glare and a hiss from his mama.

"Not everybody," said Audie.

"Not me." Sophie said it with such tiny gumption that Cooper's throat tightened. "I used to, but not anymore." She held her crutches up. "Now I got three."

Everyone laughed and the tension in the sanctuary popped like a bubble. Tess raised an eyebrow at Cooper. "That's some little girl you got there," she said, the admiration in her eyes tightening up Cooper's throat a little bit more.

"I know that," he choked out, feeling like he and Sophie had just turned an important corner. There would be a million other moments like this if they settled into Martins Gap, but there were a million moments like that even if they went back to a lifestyle where they constantly moved from place to place. The difference was they could slough them off like rainwater when they traveled from city to city. Now, since they were staying, every jab or look had a bit more weight, a bit more dig.

"I like that girl," Adele Buckton declared with a wink and a nod from a bit farther down the pew. "She knows her worth."

Settling down was best for Sophie, Cooper reminded himself. Staying was worth the price.

*I'll need to feel You beside me, Lord. Beside both of us*, Cooper prayed. *This is too large and hard to do on my own.*

When the next hymn was "Just a Closer Walk with Thee," Grace's favorite, Cooper felt his late wife smiling her blessing down on his new surroundings.

*Help me make this stick*, Cooper prayed. *Help me make this Sophie's new home.*

Tess should have known a morning at church would lead to an afternoon visit. And, in all honesty, it didn't take much arm-twisting to spend some time with the Pines when Sophie begged her to come for lunch and give her hair another French-braiding session so that it could look like Audie's. She liked the time at Cooper's place—it didn't have all the baggage that full-family gatherings on the Blue Thorn still held for her. Besides, she was getting the sense that Cooper was slowly opening up to her, and she was enjoying getting to know him better. As a Buckton, and as a woman, she had a growing urge to know what made this man tick, what he had in mind for his future.

Cooper pleaded horse chores when the girlie hair accessories came out after lunch, leaving Tess and Sophie in front of the mirror in the little girl's room.

"I'm going to love Rainbow Sparkle," Sophie said as Tess pulled a wide comb though the girl's wavy hair. "I've wanted a pet forever, but Daddy said we traveled too much."

"Pets need a place to call home. And now you'll have one, too, I hear. I'm glad you're staying."

"Me, too." She smiled at Tess in the mirror. "I like you and Audie."

Tess smiled back. "I like you, too."

"You're nice," Sophie said, fingering a set of sparkly purple hair elastics they'd selected for today's braids. "Like Dad says my mom was." Sophie swiveled her head to stare up at Tess. "Are you gonna be a mom someday?"

Poor Sophie, she had no idea what a painful question that was. Tess's first impulse was to shut down the question, but she surprised herself by deciding it was safe to talk about Bardo to her. "I wanted to be. There was a little boy back in Australia that I liked very much."

"A little boy?" Sophie's eyes grew wide. "Really?"

"He is a bit younger than you, but just as cute." With just a few words out, the need to talk about Bardo roared to life as Tess worked her fingers through Sophie's soft hair. "His name is Bardo, and he has loads of curls like you do, and great big brown eyes that could steal your heart in a second."

"Are you gonna be his mommy?"

Sophie's question stung, but not as much as Tess thought it would. She kept her eyes on the task, coaxing the story out in slow pieces. "Bardo lost his mama and his daddy, so he needed new ones. I could feel how sad and lonely he was. And he is special, just like you, because part of one arm is missing, but it doesn't slow him down one little bit. You'd like him, and he'd like you. Maybe the next time you go back to Australia you could meet him." Tess took a deep breath. "I wanted to be his mama very much."

"So will you?"

Tess remembered Gran's advice to talk about it. True, Gran probably hadn't expected Tess to pour her heart out to a six-year-old, but Sophie's guileless sweetness, with absolutely no judgment or condemnation, made it easier for the words to come out—even though she had to push them over the band of pain that cinched her chest. "I wish I could," she said. "I tried very hard to be." It healed the wound, in an odd sort of way, to put the whole complicated awful mess into terms a child could understand. *I did try very hard. Just in a multitude of foolish ways.*

"But you aren't?"

"There are lots of rules about that kind of thing," Tess explained. "Those rules won't let me be Bardo's mom." Tess wished her voice didn't catch so much on that admission. If this wasn't the first time she'd admitted that out loud to anyone, it sure felt like it.

"And so you're sad?"

Tess swallowed back a surprisingly strong threat of tears. "Yes, I'm sad. It's hard, and why I like spending time with you. It always feels better to be near people you like." She leaned in and allowed herself the pleasure of a kiss atop Sophie's curls.

Sophie laughed and replied with a pint-size

peck on Tess's hand. She tugged on that hand, bringing Tess's head close while she whispered, "Daddy likes being near you. I heard him tell Glenno he likes you too much. What does that mean? How can you like somebody too much?"

Tess felt her cheeks redden. How was she supposed to answer a question like that? How to handle what the girl had just revealed?

"Well…" Tess started braiding again while she groped for a suitable explanation. "It's more complicated for grown-ups, I suppose." It made her head spin to hear what she'd already suspected—that she wasn't the only one feeling the growing attraction between Cooper and herself. Based on Sophie's report, it was clear that she also wasn't the only one to realize it wasn't an especially good idea to act on right now.

"Do you think Daddy loves you?" Sophie giggled the question, innocent of its enormity.

Now Tess was sure her cheeks were bright pink. "Oh, Sophie, we barely know each other." That wasn't how it felt. In the same way that her connection with Bardo had run deep almost instantly, Tess felt a deep connection to Cooper. Sophie was a large part of that, but she was only part of it.

The girl scrunched up her face in confusion. "But I haven't had long to know Rainbow Sparkle and I love her already."

Tess shut her eyes for a moment, stumped. "Of course you do, but that's different."

"How?"

*Oh, Lord, grant me enough wisdom to handle this conversation.* Tess put her arms around Sophie from behind and said, "I'm sure your daddy will find someone to love someday just like he loved your mommy, and you'll all be really happy."

"Can it be you?"

Tess heart twisted as she lay her cheek atop Sophie's curls. "Oh, sweetie. It's not wrong to want a mommy again—you should have one, and I know you will someday."

"I saw him hold your hand, and I've seen lots of pictures of Daddy holding Mommy's hand. And you just said you want to be a mama to Bardo but can't. You could be mine instead."

Cooper was right—nothing escaped Sophie's eyes. She wasn't quite sure how Sophie had seen them talking in his backyard or by the Buckton barn, but obviously she had. "Your dad and I were just talking about serious things, that's all. Like I said, it's not as simple as you and Rainbow Sparkle."

Sophie swiveled on her chair to hug Tess,

and Tess tightened her hold on the little girl. The embrace fed something, filled parts of the gaping hole she'd been walking around with since Adelaide. She knew her family loved her, that Gran would always be in her corner, but something about Sophie's affection met a need Tess couldn't begin to explain. She wanted to tell the little girl she loved her—for she did, even after so short a time—but it wouldn't be wise given the conversation they'd just had. To kids, love was love. It was only grown-ups who gave it complicated forms and values.

And then there was this little girl's father. Sophie hadn't gotten the idea out of nowhere—there was something going on between the two of them. Cooper crept into her thoughts far too frequently. She'd spent much of her time on the Blue Thorn thinking about being here and seeing him again. She held the memory of his eyes and his smile far too clearly in her mind. If even a six-year-old had picked up on the connection between them, what did that say? "I'm happy just being your friend and giving you Rainbow Sparkle."

Sophie turned back toward the mirror and picked up the comb Tess had been using. "Daddy's not happy."

\* \* \*

"Daddy's not happy."

Cooper leaned against the hallway wall as he heard those words come from his daughter. He thought he'd hidden most of his stress from her, but then again he also knew how little he could conceal from Sophie. The heightened perception that made him such a successful trainer showed up in her, as well, even at this age. It burned in his gut to know Sophie realized he was unhappy.

A gut that was already in knots from the conversation he'd been overhearing. Sophie would talk to anyone about anything—it was part of the reason he had to be so careful about how people got access to her—but she also had a way of getting people to talk to her. He'd learned a mountain of things about Tess Buckton in the last five minutes that she'd kept bottled up during her earlier conversations with him. Sophie's kind and open heart did that to people. It made him wonder if his heart was in any way kind or open anymore.

"Your dad's got a lot on his mind right now," came Tess's voice. "He's planning how to be the best dad he can to you. He wants to make sure you're happy as you grow up."

"I'd be happy if you came to our family like Rainbow Sparkle did. Should I tell Daddy that?"

This couldn't be allowed to go on. Shaking himself, Cooper pushed off the hallway wall to feign walking past the doorway. "Tell Daddy what?"

His ruse failed. Tess's eyes told him she knew how much he'd heard, and he was sure his face probably broadcast the same thing. All of his innards cringed—he was up to his ears in it now, that was sure.

"Oh, nothing." Tess's eyes were wide while her cheeks were still flushed. For all the awkwardness in the room, it wasn't fair how the combination sent a hum into his chest. Half stumped, half curious, Cooper waited to see what Tess would say next. "We were talking about how Rainbow Sparkle is coming to be part of your family." Her voice held so much uncertainty the words were practically a question.

*And a whole lot more than that*, Cooper added silently. "I know you can't wait for that. Tomorrow's the big day, right?"

Sophie got up from her chair in front of the mirror and turned to flop onto her bed, a tiny heap of impatience. "I caaaan't wait," she whined. She turned her face to look up at him. "Can't she just come now? I'm ready for her, I promise."

"I don't think one more day will harm you or her," Cooper replied. "And we want Rain—" he stopped himself, annoyed that the silly name was about to roll of his tongue "—your kitten to have a chance to say good-bye to her mama cat and siblings, now, don't we?"

He was trying not to look at Tess's eyes, but it was as if he couldn't stop himself. She knew what he'd said to Glenno about his growing feelings for her. It made everything so much more…complicated.

*See what happens when you talk about your feelings even the tiniest bit? It never fails to get out of hand.*

"Miss Tess has a little boy she wants to come into her family. From Australia, like us. Only he can't."

He hadn't heard that part of the conversation. The pink in Tess's cheeks disappeared, replaced by a humiliated paleness. She practically shrank in on herself right in front of him, wide-eyed and exposed.

"Oh?" was all he could bring himself to say. Here she was coaxing him to reveal his plans while she kept quiet about something as big as a pending adoption? Or wait—Sophie had said "can't." Could this be part of the mess she'd alluded to earlier? He ought to be irritated that she'd kept secrets, but instead he just felt for the painful, vulnerable look all over her face right now. "We'll have to talk about that more later."

*No, we won't,* said Tess's panicked features. "It's time for me to go. Your hair's done," she blurted out.

"No…" Sophie cried, clinging to Tess.

"I'm sure you and your daddy have lots of things to do," Tess said, moving toward the door but looking like she didn't like that it brought her closer to him.

Sophie's lower lip stuck out. "I did it again, didn't I? Said stuff I wasn't s'posed to?"

He and Tess exchanged excruciated glances. "We'll talk about it later," Cooper said. The level of awkward in the air practically made his skin itch.

Sophie looked up at Tess. "He always says that when I'm in trouble."

"You just need to learn—"

"Discretion," he and Sophie said at the same time. "I don't get why everyone's so mad."

"I'm not mad," Tess said. "Just…" She threw another I-don't-know-what-to-say look at Cooper. "I'll just go." She waved to Sophie and tried to angle herself through the door as he stepped aside to give her room. "I'll see you tomorrow, sweetie. It'll be a fun day, I promise."

"I'll walk Miss Tess out," Cooper told his daughter. "You put away your toys now and we'll talk in a bit."

The last thing he wanted to do was follow Tess Buckton right now, but there was no way he could leave the conversation where it was. Tess was currently rivaling Sophie's pace for barreling down the hallway. He caught her by the elbow just before she made it to the door, and she whirled on him, eyes wide and glistening with tears.

He let go of Tess's elbow, stunned and embarrassed to see her so openly distraught. "Can we talk about what just happened?"

Tess wrapped her arms around her chest. "No."

"Was what Sophie said right? You tried to adopt a child in Australia and couldn't?"

Tess pulled in a breath and looked up to the ceiling, clearly fighting to keep those brimming tears from spilling over. "I don't want to talk about it."

"You told Sophie. You could tell her and not me?" That came out more accusatory than he would have liked, but this was the woman who'd spent days trying to get his own secrets out of him.

He made himself soften his voice. "Is this the mistake you were talking about?" He didn't see how something as noble as trying to adopt a child could turn into the searing wound she described. And yet…she'd said her mistakes had stemmed from love, hadn't she? He didn't know anything about adoptions or how they could go wrong, but it wasn't hard to connect the dots Sophie had given him.

"It's nothing. I'm sorry I said anything." She put her hand on the doorknob.

He put his hand against the door. "Come on, Tess, it's not nothing. I'm sorry she blurted it out, but tell me the rest of it, will you?"

Tess stood still. "There's nothing to tell. You heard it. I tried to adopt in Adelaide but I…couldn't."

"There's more to it than that." It didn't take any perceptive skills to see that.

"Nothing else worth telling." Tess pulled open the door. "I'll see you tomorrow." She lowered her voice. "The doll arrived at the ranch yesterday. I'll give it to her tomorrow with the kitten. I know she'll love both of them."

Cooper looked at this woman, so much love bottled up that she was pouring it out on his own daughter after mere weeks of knowing her, and felt his heart ache in a long-forgotten way. An ache he wasn't entirely sure he'd ever feel again and certainly not one he was willing to trust. Not now, at least. Tess was clearly in the throes of recovering from some mess, and he was about to launch into one of his own. The only thing that could make everything worse would be to rush head-long into something that could go so awfully wrong and hurt all three of them.

Whatever this thing was between them, it could wait. It *should* wait. But as he closed the door behind Tess, his own words to Glenno came back to him. *I like her too much. Too much to let her go, and too much to keep her close.*

Between Rainbow Sparkle and Tess's doll gift on Monday, and a crucial meeting with the bank on Tuesday, it was going to be killer pair of days.

# Chapter Ten

Cooper was still in a bad mood when his mobile phone rang an hour later. "Do you know how hard you are to get a hold of these days?" Hunter's voice had the tinny shout of a busy man on his car phone.

Cooper swallowed. He'd hesitated for a moment when Hunter's name came up on the phone screen before deciding to answer. *I can't avoid him forever. I shouldn't avoid him at all.* "I'm supposed to be on holiday, mate."

Hunter's idea of holiday was probably cutting business calls down to fifty a day. "Break's almost over," his brother justified. "I emailed the next season's preliminary schedule to you nearly a week ago. What do you think?"

Cooper sat back on his desk chair, casting a glance at the very full inbox on his email program. "Again, mate, Sunday? Holiday? Look it up in the dictionary."

"It's Monday here."

Monday or not, what was Hunter doing starting plans for the next season already? Cooper shouldn't wait to pull the plug any longer, but he didn't have it in him to tackle this today. Not after this afternoon's fiasco with Sophie and Tess. "Look, I…"

"My flight lands at one-thirty Wednesday. Can you fetch me from the airport?"

Cooper sat up straight. "I thought you were coming back on the eighteenth."

"Wrapped up early. Ahead of schedule and under budget."

Well, at least Hunter would be in a good mood when Cooper pulled the rug out from underneath him. "Not hard to do when you save a ton of time and tape footage not having to film arguments between us."

Hunter laughed. "Discussions. And the world loves our discussions."

"*You* love our arguments. You just *think* everyone else does." So Hunter was coming here in a matter of days. Maybe it had been God's grace that he'd avoided the declaration of his future plans until now. It would be better, more honest, to have this conversation face-to-face. Maybe even in the SUV on the way home from the airport where no one could stomp off mad and Sophie would be out of earshot for the first angry volleys of fire. "Sure, I'll fetch."

He was about to say something about getting the spare bedroom ready when Hunter went on. "I've got dinner meetings in San Antonio but we can have a late lunch in Austin and go over things, right?"

That was Hunter—available, but never for long. Still, it might be a good way to do it. If he told Hunter in a public place, with a finite amount of time to hash it out, there'd be no chance of things coming to blows with his hyper-image-conscious brother. He was pretty sure they wouldn't, anyway, but there was no knowing how badly Hunter would take this. Especially if he'd already started drawing up next season's details—this was early, even for him.

"How's the birthday girl? Did she get my present?"

Cooper sighed. He'd shown the gift to Sophie, but hadn't really given it to her. "A six-year-old does not need her own mobile, Hunter. What's she going to do with a fancy smartphone like that?" In truth, Sophie had played with it for about half an hour and then moved on to something else. He hadn't gone through the process of connecting the expensive device to his phone plan. Had Hunter forgotten how much he disliked mobiles? Or simply ignored it?

Hunter laughed. "Didn't you see? You control who she can call. It's a special mobile for kids her age."

*There should be no mobiles for kids her age*, Cooper thought, pinching the bridge of his nose. He didn't much care for the world nudging Sophie toward the teen years before she was even ten. She was a challenge to handle even now, as this afternoon had clearly showed. He couldn't even begin to imagine a teenage Sophie. He'd have gray hair and an ulcer by then, surely.

"There are four of the best pre-reading apps already installed for her to play with and learn stuff. Come on, mate, let her call me. We can send photos back and forth. We can video chat."

Cooper had wanted Sophie to have more connection with Hunter, and it would mostly have to be by phone when he left the show. Hunter might stop speaking to him, but he'd never freeze out Sophie. Maybe the mobile was more of a blessing than he realized, even for a disinterested six-year-old. It'd take him all of twenty minutes to set it up on his phone plan. He was going to be at the bank tomorrow finalizing the financing for Pine Purpose Ranch, and it'd give Sophie something interesting to do while he was gone. She could send Hunter videos of the new kitten and photos of the doll Tess was giving her.

That caught him up short for a minute. His brother, who'd known Sophie for years, had given her a gift that made almost no sense at all. Tess, who'd known Sophie for weeks, was giving her two of the best gifts he could ever imagine for his little girl. That said something, something he should pay attention to, but he wasn't entirely sure what that was.

"Okay, mate," he said into the phone. "I'll put the mobile on my plan, show her how to ring you up, and the two of you can chat up a storm Tuesday afternoon while I'm…in town on errands." *Errands at the bank to finalize my mortgage to buy a ranch and set up a therapy program you don't know about.* He'd learn soon enough. "Can you wake up for Sophie if she calls around one in the afternoon, our time?" Let Uncle Hunter see how "smart" his smartphone was to be taking calls on Sophie's hours.

"No worries, mate, I'll already be up. My flight's at six a.m. Wednesday my time."

Crazy intercontinental time zones—Hunter

could calculate them in a heartbeat, but Cooper was weary of them. "She's got a fun play date tomorrow and she can tell you all about it when she calls." Tess and Audie and a kitten and a doll constituted a play date, right? Just as long as it didn't constitute an actual date that included him, they'd be okay.

"I'll set my alarm, get my packing done early."

"You do that."

There was a pause on the other end of the line before Hunter added, "You okay?"

Cooper stilled, not ready to be exposed for the second time today. "Why?"

"You sound... I don't know, off."

Hunter was handing him an open door. He wasn't ready to walk through it. "I've been thinking about a lot of things."

"Too much time on your hands out there in the middle of nowhere. You pick the most boring holidays, brother."

Hunter's idea of an acceptable holiday usually involved risking life and limb in crazy activities like surfing and rock climbing and even skydiving.

"I want to talk about next season, Hunter."

"Why do you think I'm coming in early? You should see the ideas I've got cooked up. We're gonna have so much fun. Pine Camp—

do you love it? A week-long retreat for Pineys and their horses. With a minicamp for kids. If it takes off, we can open a whole resort division. I'll bring all the details on Wednesday."

There was going to be no easing into this. He was going to have to hit Hunter over the head with the pronouncement of his departure. Cut things off in no uncertain terms. Cooper couldn't bring himself to do that over the phone. He slumped back into the chair. "Yeah, we'll talk Wednesday. But I want you to listen to me when we talk things over, okay? No just me saying yes to your ideas."

"Hey, I always listen."

Hunter rarely listened. Hunter went full-speed ahead with what he "knew" was best for the pair of them. Of course, Hunter was often right, and had built the business into a huge empire, so it was hard to disagree with the guy.

Except on this. This was the one time Cooper absolutely knew *he* was right, and he would have to stand his ground until Hunter came around. And hope and pray that Hunter did come around.

"See you one-thirty Wednesday. You'll hear from Sophie Tuesday afternoon—well, Wednesday morning for you. G'day, then."

"G'day, Coop. See you Wednesday."

Cooper ended the call, feeling as if he'd just set the end of a whole part of his life in motion. And he had. If everything went well Tuesday at the bank, Pine Purpose Ranch would come to be within weeks. The plans would be under way by the time he saw Hunter, so there'd be no backing out. Once Hunter knew, once Cooper kept his promise to himself that Hunter would hear it from him and before everyone else, then the whole world could know about Pine Purpose Ranch. Or not. The choice would be his, not coordinated by some ratings-hungry marketing team. He'd be his own man with his own life to live on his own terms.

It was a good thing. A start God had made clear to him months ago. A first step toward the life he wanted for Sophie and for himself.

So why did it feel like everything was a tangled mess out of his control?

Tess had the box from Delight Toys open on the kitchen table when Jana Buckton knocked on the front door of the ranch house Monday morning. "Witt's down at the store, so I thought I'd bring up the new food truck menu samples to Gunner. Is he here?"

The lead Blue Thorn Burgers food truck chef was a petite, pretty woman with compelling eyes and a mass of brown curly hair. She made an excellent addition to the Buckton family by Tess's standards. Smart, strong, talented, and with a mean coleslaw recipe in tow.

"He's out in the pastures. Can I see?"

"Sure." She handed Tess the mock-ups, but then cast her eyes on the box containing Sophie's doll. "What's this?"

"A special doll for Cooper Pine's daughter. With crutches and a prosthetic leg. I met the woman who makes them on a flight a few months ago, and when Sophie mentioned that none of her dolls look like her, I knew I had to call."

Jana picked up the box. "That's sweet. Really. I always wanted a doll that looked like me growing up. They never quite came with all this curly hair, so I used to try curling it." She shook her wild mane. "Never worked. Mostly I just melted the doll's hair right off. I make a better cook than I do a beautician."

"Sophie will be thrilled when I give it to her this afternoon, don't you think?"

"I'm sure. You met them in Australia, I take it? Before they came here?"

"No. I met Cooper in Lolly's the day I landed." Tess felt odd admitting the short time she'd known Cooper.

Jana's expression said the same as she looked at the Canadian return address on the packaging. "So you just up and got this for Sophie? After knowing them such a short time?"

"I know. It's not weird or anything, is it?"

Jana put the box down. "Do you feel weird about it?"

Tess ran her hand along the box. "My heart just sort of locked on to Sophie right away. When she made that remark about none of her dolls looking like her, and I knew the woman who made these, it felt like one of those 'God moments' Gran always talks about."

"And her dad? He's okay with it?" Jana sat.

Tess joined her at the table. "I think so. I did ask him before I ordered it. The company donates them, so it's not like I spent a ton of money or anything. Just express shipping… and a surcharge for the rush order."

"Her dad is kind of famous, isn't he? Witt and I watched the show on television the other day. You'd think he'd have already arranged for a doll like this himself."

"I wanted to be the one to do it," Tess defended.

"Does this have anything to do with Sophie's handsome dad?"

"No."

"It's okay if it does, you know. You can care about that little girl and have feelings for her father at the same time."

"A relationship is the last thing I'm looking for," Tess argued. "And I'd guess that Cooper feels the same way."

"Hey, I'm not judging. I had a hundred reasons not to get involved with Witt, and it happened despite every one of them. You know, maybe the doll isn't the only 'God thing' going on here."

Tess felt her cheeks flush. "He's Cooper Pine. The man has a fan cub. I'm definitely not looking to line up behind his legions of fans."

Jana smiled. "Brooke said he looked like a fan of yours at the barbecue. And Sophie adores you."

The way Cooper had looked at her had indeed healed some of the wounds left from Jasper.

Cooper Pine's eyes conveyed honor and respect instead of the over-the-top romance from Jasper that turned out to be not only false but predatory. Was her attraction a function of Cooper's integrity? Or her own damaged rebound? She couldn't say, and that meant she had to keep a careful distance from the man if not from his daughter.

"I think he did have a good time at the barbecue—at least until Gunner and Luke gave him a grilling about his plans for the Larkey ranch," she retorted. "His plans are going to keep him too busy for anything but his home and his family, and I've decided that I'm treading carefully where Cooper Pine is concerned."

"Well, if that man isn't grateful beyond words for what you're doing for Sophie, he needs his head examined. I'm sorry I won't be there when you give it to her—I imagine it'll be the most heartwarming thing most of us have seen in a long time."

Tess put the wrapping back over the box. "I sure hope so."

## Chapter Eleven

Cooper and Sophie arrived later that afternoon and the "kitten extravaganza"—as Audie, who was delighted to have that Monday off from school, put it—was going well. This second visit to the Blue Thorn Ranch was going much better than the first, and Tess couldn't remember when she'd felt so happy and satisfied. Sophie was over the moon about finally getting to take Rainbow Sparkle home for good, and Tess hoped the present in the box she held would double the little girl's joy.

"Here, Sophie, I've got a surprise for you." She set the large cardboard box down on the living room floor while several of the family members and Cooper looked on.

"For me? But I already got a kitty."

"I know, but this is something special I could do for you."

Cooper crouched down beside his daughter. "Surely you want to wait and open this at home," he teased.

Sophie clutched at the box. "No! I wanna open it right now. Can I? Can I, please?"

Sophie began tearing at the outer wrapping to reveal a brightly striped inner box. Tess watched her pull apart the tissue and gasp in wonder when the face of a doll smiled up from under the plastic window.

"Daddy!" Sophie nearly squealed. "A doll! And her hair is my color. And her eyes, too!"

The doll did resemble Sophie with her eyes and bouncy strawberry-blond curls. But Tess knew it also resembled Sophie in the way that truly mattered. She watched Cooper's amazed expression, feeling Sophie's wonder in the pit of her own stomach as her father helped her lift off the lid of the box.

Tess could see and feel the moment when Sophie realized the doll had a prosthetic leg. A very pink, very girly, prosthetic leg. Sophie went quiet, awestruck even, and slowly reached out to touch the artificial limb. Would Sophie love it or hate it? Suddenly all Tess's certainty that this had been the right thing to do vanished under the fear that she'd made a terrible mistake. She'd overstepped and over-loved, again.

Sophie turned to Cooper, her eyes wide in shock. Wonder? Or horror? "She's just like me," Sophie whispered. "Daddy, she's *just* like me."

Gran sniffed, and Ruby, Luke's physical therapist fiancée who had asked to come see the special gift, put a hand on Tess's shoulder. Tess thought she would puddle up in relief right there on the spot. Cooper's eyes were filled with astonishment and gratitude and a million other things as he looked at Tess—a look that shot through her like lightning.

Sophie picked up the doll and held her up as if to show the whole world. "She's just like me," she repeated, grinning at the whole room of onlookers. "Look at her pink leg, Daddy. Look at it." She ran her hand down the admittedly space-age-looking prosthesis and the matching bright pink tennis shoes.

When she hugged the doll, eyes shut tight in tiny six-year-old delight, Tess saw Cooper choke back tears. "There's some other stuff in here," he said thickly, needing something to do to cover the surge of emotion felt by everyone in the room. "Should we look?"

Another box revealed a miniature set of

crutches—also pink—and a pair of white cowboy boots.

"You're not going to make me run to the hardware store for a can of pink spray paint for your crutches or anything, are you, sunshine?" He was fighting hard to keep his composure, and it sank indelibly into Tess's heart.

"Yeah, you could have your own pink crutches just like these," Audie agreed, taking the doll's pair as Sophie handed them to her.

Tess wiped away the stream of tears wetting her cheek as Sophie repeated, "She's just like me. Look at her leg, Audie. She's just like me."

"That's a pretty snazzy piece of hardware there," Cooper choked out, pointing to the prosthetic.

"It's not quite like mine." Tess had seen the limb in Sophie's closet. The way Sophie said the words told Tess that the existing leg would never compare to the doll's space-age limb. Had she made a mistake in that?

Cooper had followed the same train of thought. "Would you want one like that?"

"Maybe." She bent the knee a few times more. "Then I could carry stuff like Rainbow Sparkle. And Molly."

"Who's Molly?"

"She is. I decided, just now." She turned Molly to face Cooper, as if making a formal introduction.

Cooper reached out to the small plastic hand Sophie extended. "G'day, Molly. Pleased to meet ya."

"Molly, meet Audie." The girls were instantly lost in an enthusiastic exploration of all the doll's accessories and positions. Tess felt their laughter wash over her like a healing rain. It was an amazing relief to do this one important thing right after slogging through so many wrongs.

Cooper rose and walked over to Tess, his eyes glistening. "I don't know what to say. I don't know how to thank you."

She smiled. It felt so good to smile. "What I just saw was thanks enough."

Cooper looked like he wanted to say more but couldn't get any other words out past the lump in his throat she knew rivaled her own. Tess reached out and squeezed his hand to let him know she understood. "I saw the prosthetic leg in her closet. I hope I haven't made things worse by giving her unrealistic expectations."

"Not at all," Cooper choked out, gaining back some of his composure with a topic of conversation. "Hers is nowhere near as fancy as that—but there are fancier ones on the market. We never looked into them because there didn't seem to be a point, given that she's never really bothered with the one she has."

"It's hard work to accustom her limb to the device," said Ruby, who as a therapist would know about such things.

"I think she sees it as more bother than her crutches," Cooper added. "She rarely uses it, and I rather like that she feels complete without it."

"That speaks a lot to you as a father," Ruby said, offering a smile.

"Her doctors, the ones that had fitted it? They tell me they're fine with how she ignores it. She'd need different ones as she grew, and we all are pretty sure she'll ask for a new one when she is ready."

"I'm pretty sure she'll be fixing to ask for one now," Gran said with a chuckle.

Cooper rubbed the back of his neck with one hand. "Why'd…why'd you go to all this trouble?"

"Because I could," Tess said, and it was true. She'd felt helpless and faulty for so long, it made all the difference in the world to do this, to make Sophie happy, if she couldn't do anything about Bardo.

"That's my sweet, bighearted Tess," Gran said, nodding toward the girls. "I think I'll be smiling for a week remembering this little scene."

Cooper was having a hard time keeping his emotions in check, and Tess felt for him. "How about we get some air for a minute?" she suggested.

Gran nodded. "You do that. I'll go see if there are any brownies left in the kitchen. If this doesn't call for a celebration, I don't know what does."

"I'll help," said Ruby, winking at Tess. "You two go sit on the porch for a minute. The girls'll be just fine here."

Cooper leaned up against a porch pillar and gulped down air. He hadn't felt this grateful and overwhelmed since the doctor had come out of the surgery to tell him Sophie had come through the amputation operation successfully. That had been only two days after Grace's death, and he'd nearly drowned in grief and worry that day. Today was a whole other kind of overflow, and he was at a loss for how to handle it.

He was aware of Tess behind him, but couldn't turn to face her until he somehow came up with the words to thank her. *Lord, give me the words*, he prayed, closing his eyes and reveling in the laughter he heard coming from behind the door where Sophie and Audie were. *Give me wisdom. I'm undone here.*

"I'm so glad," she said after a little while.

He turned, stunned by her remark. She was glad? What he felt went miles beyond glad, went a dozen different places besides glad. He wasn't good at this kind of thing—it was one of the reasons he valued his privacy. People were always doing nice things for him because of who he was. This went so much farther than that. It unraveled him down to his bones. It endeared Tess to him in ways he wasn't sure he could handle.

"I…" His throat tightened and his brain refused to work. His heart, however, was working overtime, thundering beneath his ribs.

"Hey," she said, walking toward him. "It's okay. I know."

Did she? Could she possible fathom the depth of what she'd done? Of all the places Cooper hoped for acceptance and connection in Martins Gap, the Buckton family ranch was the last place he'd thought to receive it.

It wasn't smart. It wasn't safe. But it wasn't anything he could stop himself from doing as he simply held up one arm and pulled Tess in next to him.

She hesitated for a second, resistance and wariness darkening her eyes, but then a careful smile slid across her lips and she offered him a hug. It had been such a terribly long time since he'd felt safe in the arms of a woman that a single, unstoppable half sob, half sigh escaped him before he could catch it back. He stiffened, embarrassed, and put one hand over his eyes as she stepped a bit back.

"It's okay," she said, wiping her eyes. "Really, I was glad to do it. I needed to do it, if that makes any sense."

He couldn't reply. If he spoke now he'd say all kinds of things that would open floodgates he was barely keeping in check as it was.

"Haven't people done nice things for Sophie before?"

Nice things. It was almost amusing how Tess categorized this colossal gesture as a "nice thing."

"I don't let many people near her," he managed to get out after a pause. "I don't... I couldn't bear it if they pitied her or used her, you know?" He managed a damp, dark laugh. "You'd be amazed what some Pineys have tried just to get to me or Hunter."

Tess sat on the porch front step. "I'm thinking I don't want to know."

"You don't." He sat on the step, as well—close, but not too close. This overwhelming urge to touch her, to hold her hand or to pull her back into the crook of his arm was making it hard to put sentences together. "It's why Sophie and Grace never appeared or were mentioned on the show." He paused before saying in lower tones, "It's why I'm leaving."

Tess turned to look at him. "You're leaving Martins Gap?" After a second she realized what he'd really meant and whispered, "Wait a minute—you're saying that you're leaving the show, aren't you? That's what you can't reveal, that's why you won't say what you're doing with the land, because no one at the show knows yet."

Cooper didn't reply, he merely nodded.

"How is Hunter taking the fact that you're leaving?"

Cooper looked at her, feeling his shoulders sinking at the unspoken admission.

Her face changed as the pieces clicked. "Hunter doesn't even know you're planning to leave," she said slowly. "You haven't told him yet."

Cooper ran one hand through his hair. "He's flying in on Wednesday, and I'm picking him up at the airport. I'm planning to tell him then. But I'm not fooling myself with any idea that he'll take it well. I'm breaking up the Pine Brothers—there isn't a bigger sin I could commit in Hunter's eyes. I'm not quite sure he'll ever forgive me. I don't want Sophie to grow up in the spotlight of the Pine Method, but I don't want to lose her uncle Hunter, either."

"Luke and I haven't always seen eye to eye, but I don't think there's anything I could do that would risk losing him altogether. Surely, Hunter will come around, won't he?"

Cooper looked out over the pastures where he could just see the silhouettes of the Buckton bison wandering through the grasses. "He sees it as the family business. He fully intends to pass it on to Sophie and his kids…whenever he has them." He turned to look at Tess. "I just can't say if he wants Sophie to be a Pine or a poster child."

"He might surprise you. But, either way, he deserves to know. I'm sure it'll be hard, but you'll get through telling him, I'm sure of it."

Easy for her to say. Everyone saw the charming, rugged side of Hunter. Privately the man could be driven, even cut-throat to anyone who got in the way of his grand plans. "Well, I'm not sure."

"Whatever you've got planned next will be worth it."

Suddenly the promise he'd made to himself to tell Hunter first seemed misguided. Hadn't the last hour proved to him that Tess could be trusted with his plans? In truth, a large part of him wanted to tell her, wanted to talk all about it and watch her reaction before he went into battle against Hunter.

He looked into her eyes and took a deep breath. He'd thought he'd have to force the words out, but in all honesty it was more like he could no longer hold them back.

"A horse therapy program," he said. "Pine Purpose Ranch will be an equine therapy facility for kids like Sophie."

Tess took a minute to absorb what he'd said. "That's what you want to do with the land?"

"I made a promise to myself that beyond Glenno and Sophie, I wouldn't tell anyone before I told Hunter." He lowered his head. "I guess I just broke that promise. With you."

She sighed, wrapping her hands around her knees as they sat together on the steps. "I don't know what I was expecting, but that sure wasn't it."

"A far cry from the Pine Method circus. None of that nonsense will be coming here—

I meant what I said that your family has nothing to worry about. It's me and my family that are at risk, not your community's peace of mind."

Tess shifted to face him. "It's such a worthy cause. How could Hunter possibly object?"

"I don't think he would, if I ran it on the side and stayed with the show. He'd probably find some way to tie it into the show. Do a fund-raising drive for scholarships, get equipment donated…and turn it into another Pine enterprise." He paused before adding, "I don't want Sophie's life to be a Pine enterprise. I've made enough mistakes when it comes to her as it is."

"But you've kept her out of the spotlight. You've been a good and careful father."

That made him laugh. "No, I'm not. I'm a mess of a man trying to make something of a life that's been jumbled to pieces. I thought I could keep it just us two, but it can't ever be just us two, can it? She's got to have a full, stable life with a steady home and friends and a kitten and…" He shook his head. "Some days I feel like if I look away for even a second she'll be driving, and then married, and without Hunter I'll be alone." He straightened. "See what I mean about a jumbled mess?"

Tess placed her hand on top of his. "You're

not much of a mess from where I sit. Sophie's blessed to have a dad like you. And even if Hunter never speaks to you again, Martins Gap can be your family. People here won't leave you alone."

Cooper's hand turned over to clasp Tess's. "I've kind of noticed folks in Martins Gap don't leave me alone."

Tess flushed. "That's not what I meant."

"There's left alone and there's *all* alone. I want Sophie and I to be left alone to be a family—not a show stunt or some kind of spectacle to gawk at—but I don't want us to be all alone." He squeezed her hand. "I'm asking you not to say anything about my plans, even to your family, until I can talk to Hunter. I need to try and keep what's left of that promise to make sure he doesn't hear about my plans from anyone else."

"Would you like me to take Sophie when you talk to him?"

He smiled. "No, Glenno can take care of that." He looked down. He was holding hands with Tess Buckton. The risk of it made his skin tingle and his heart jump, but the connection seemed to soothe the empty place he'd carried for years. He ought to drop her hand before anyone came out and saw, but he couldn't quite talk himself into it.

"Tell me how it goes?" she said, squeezing his hand. "I'll say a prayer for you."

"Say twenty, will you? Between Hunter and this meeting I have at the bank tomorrow, I'll need them all."

"Sure I—"

Her reply was cut short by a whoop from inside the house. Tess's grandmother came out, Ruby right behind her. "Nash just called," she cried, waving her hands in the air. "The twins are on their way!"

## Chapter Twelve

Wednesday morning, Hunter thrust his bags into the back of Cooper's SUV and slammed the trunk with a furious force. From the look on his face, he must have had a horrific flight. Cooper's meeting with the bank yesterday afternoon hadn't been a barrel of laughs, either, and the likelihood of this crucial lunch going well was heading downhill with every passing minute.

Hunter practically threw himself into the passenger seat and whammed the door shut with a grunt. "Drive," he growled, not even looking at Cooper.

"Hello to you, too." Cooper tried not to snarl back. "Bad flight?"

"You could say that." He stewed in silence for a few minutes as Cooper maneuvered away from the terminal, then suddenly

Hunter pointed to the parking lot a few yards away and said, "Pull over."

Cooper looked at him. "What?"

"I said pull over. I don't want to do this while you're driving."

Cooper felt the hairs on the back of his neck stand up. The air in the cabin grew thick as he swerved the vehicle off the ramp and into one corner of the lot.

Within seconds of the SUV coming to a stop, Hunter shifted toward him, anger sharpening his features. He cursed, something Hunter didn't do very often, before demanding to know, "What are you doing?"

"I'm fetching you off your flight, mate." Cooper tried not to grind the words through his teeth. After yesterday, he should be spending this afternoon fetching all the ridiculous new documentation the bank, attorneys, brokers and zoning commission had demanded. The deal was supposed to be nearly done by now. Instead of giving him the foundation to get through today, it had been an infuriating, frustrating meeting. He had precious little slack to cut his snarky older brother for barking questions at him like this.

"You've messed it all up. Everything!" Hunter shouted. "And you didn't even have the decency to tell me. I have to learn you're leaving the show for some stupid notion from Sophie? *Sophie?* That's how much you think of everything we've built?"

Cooper's pulse halted. He'd been so preoccupied with the outcome of yesterday's bank meeting he hadn't asked Sophie for any details on how her phone conversation with Hunter had gone.

Things had officially gone from irritating to disastrous. Suddenly there wasn't enough grace on the planet to get him through the next few hours. "What did Sophie tell you?"

"Oh, Sophie had loads to say. That you're not just on vacation. That you're staying there 'forever.'" Hunter started waving his hands around the way he did when he was truly steamed. "That she got a new kitten from your neighbor. That she wants a leg like her doll's—whatever that means. That you're starting a 'horses that help' ranch. That you're leaving the show. That she's getting a new mommy." He stilled, eyes burning into Cooper's. "I could go on, but I think that's enough to start on, don't you?"

Cooper's brain was reeling, trying to take stock of what had just happened. If he'd tried to think up the worst way for Hunter to find out, this topped anything he could have imagined. "Whoa, hang on there."

"I will not 'hang on there.' No wonder you dragged your feet giving Sophie the mobile. You knew she'd spill everything, and you wanted to keep your harebrained plans secret for as long as you could. I can think of a lot of people I'd suspect of holding out on me, but you? You? I don't even know where to start. I don't even know what to think." Hunter glared at Cooper. "Were you ever going to tell me?"

Cooper didn't know where to start, either. "I was going to tell you today. I knew you wouldn't take it well. That you'd get mad."

"Mad?" Hunter's voice rose further. "Insult my car, call me names, then I get mad. Pull the rug out from underneath the show with no notice like you're skipping out on some kind of restaurant reservation? I'm miles beyond mad." Hunter wiped his hands down his face. "Crikey, Coop, how long have you been planning this?"

Cooper didn't really have an answer. "I've been…wanting to leave for…a while." Each word felt like it was launching a knife into Hunter's chest—and twisting his own stomach into a tighter knot. "The idea for a therapy ranch came to me a bit back, and I knew it was what I wanted to do. I just didn't know when or how." He leaned his head back against the seat and cut the ignition. "I know you needed to know—to be the first to know—I just couldn't figure out a way to tell you."

Hunter shifted again to face him, brow furrowed, hands fisted. "I cut you a lot of slack. When Grace died, I carried you because that's what brothers do." His words grew darker and sharper with every sentence. "I made excuses for you until you got your feet back underneath you and then I made sure there was a place for you to come back. I had your back. I made sure you were part of everything. And now...now I wonder if I even want to save you from the mess you're about to make. Why should I even bother? It's not like you've given me any reason to warn you."

Cooper was still trying to catch up from everything Hunter said. "The therapy ranch is not some 'mess' I'm about to make. I know what I'm doing and why I'm doing it."

"Oh, I could care less right now about you going all warm and fuzzy with your pony helpers or whatever it is you're up to. The lady, though—well, that's a whole other story."

In all the shock of Hunter finding out about the ranch, Cooper hadn't even gotten to Sophie's proclamation of her "new mama."

"Sophie's got the wrong idea about Tess and me."

"Oh, I don't think so. She told me all about the lady next door who's been by all the time, who brought her a kitten and a doll with one leg and all the other stuff. 'Daddy really likes her and she really likes Daddy.' Do you even know anything about Tess Buckton? At all?"

Some corner of Cooper's brain registered the fact that Hunter knew her name as a bad thing. "She's been great to Sophie. To me."

Hunter's laugh was dark and slippery. "Oh, I'm sure she has. A regular little wonder right next door. You're being played, Cooper. Again. Wake up."

"What do you mean?"

"What has she told you about herself?"

Cooper didn't like that he drew a blank on his answer. "Enough. I'm not in the habit of asking for background checks."

"Maybe you should. Did you know she's been in Adelaide?"

"I did. What are you getting at, Hunter?"

"I figured someone'd try this sooner or later. I just thought it'd be a Piney, not the girl next door."

Cooper flexed his fists against the steering wheel. "What are you getting at?" he repeated.

"I always figured you to be smart enough

to catch when someone's after your money. I did a little digging on the plane after Sophie told me all kinds of lovey-dovey tales about how much Tess was doing for you. The visits, the presents, the sad story of the little orphan boy she told Sophie." Hunter put his hand satirically to his chest. "Heartbreaking."

He'd heard only the tail end of Tess's conversation with Sophie, and Hunter had hit a sore spot. It did bother him that Tess had confided in Sophie but not in him. It had irked him that he still didn't know the whole story and yet Hunter and even Sophie knew more. He pushed open the door and began pacing around the parking lot pavement, angry, confused and with a niggling suspicion that made him sick to his stomach.

Hunter got out of the SUV and stared at him over the hood. "Tell me you knew."

"I knew she'd hit a rough patch in Adelaide." It sounded as feeble as it felt.

"A rough patch. Yeah, I'd call it that." Hunter planted his hands on the SUV's hood and leaned in toward Cooper. "She's up to her eyeballs in debt, mate, and you're the solution with deep pockets who just moved in next door. She owes money to some very nasty blokes who aren't known for their patience. And all to fund an adoption that was never going to happen. Really, what idiot thinks the Department of Human Services would hand over an aboriginal orphan to some single twenty-five-year-old American? I'd say the guy who took her money knew a good mark when he saw one and—"

"That's enough!" Cooper shouted, turning away. He turned back a second later. "Where'd you get all these…?" He wanted to say "lies," but he couldn't. The little ember of doubt began burning a larger hole in his gut.

"After my little chat with Sophie where all the alarm bells went off in my head, I did a little digging. A fifteen-hour flight with internet access and a few well-placed emails to friends gave me a chance to fill in the blanks."

"Hunter, you think you have rights to the whole world's business some days."

Hunter threw his hands up. "Well, forgive me for trying to protect my family. *Someone* had to do the thinking for you and Sophie— you sure weren't."

Cooper didn't even know what to say. Half of him wanted to get in the SUV and leave Hunter stranded in the Austin airport parking lot. The other half of him wanted to go through Hunter's computer and see all the crazy accusations spelled out.

His heart was yelling it couldn't be true. After all his caution, the walls he'd wisely built around himself and Sophie to keep them safe from anyone trying to take advantage, Tess had to have broken through because of her true caring. He was starting to believe that Tess really was the woman who could heal his heart that had been in useless pieces for so long.

His brain was the traitor, hinting that what Hunter said made a painful sort of sense. He knew she'd had problems and that she was struggling with shame over what had happened. Was this the part of the story she'd refused to admit?

"Tell me she told you. Tell me she's come clean about the kind of money trouble she's in and that she hasn't been cozying up to you way more than makes sense."

Cooper didn't answer because he couldn't. "It can't be."

"Sure it can," Hunter barked back. "It already has. That's the thing that bugs me most, mate. This is worse than Lynette. I can't believe you didn't see this for what it is."

"You're wrong about her."

Hunter crossed his arms over his chest. "I don't think so. I verified my facts. I had a long flight to cross-check all the dirty little details. I called in a few favors *on your be-half, brother*, because we're family and that's *supposed* to mean something."

Cooper stared at his brother. "I should have told you. I get that."

"Yes." Hunter practically ground the word out through his teeth.

"I'm sorry." Despite the storm careening around his head, he could at least get that much out.

"Don't bail on the show, Coop." Hunter softened his voice only slightly—it still felt like a demand. "It's a huge mistake. No one knows about any of these crazy therapy ranch plans yet, we can shut it down right here before it goes further. Buy the place, settle down if you want. Make it a home, not a business, and get to work with me on the next season of the show. We'll figure it out. We always have."

"No, *you* always have. I know what I want, Hunter. I didn't go about it right but that doesn't change my decision. I want out."

"You don't. You're just tired. This woman's got your head messed up."

Tess may have his heart messed up, and he was going to have to talk to her about what he'd just learned, but that didn't change Pine Purpose Ranch's future. That had been decided long before Tess entered the picture. "I want out, Hunter. No more tours, no more tapings, no more travel."

"So we'll change the schedule. Cut your travel down by half, maybe even two-thirds. Bring Sophie to the camp thing, bring her everywhere on set if you want so you never have to be away from her for long. We'll hire a tutor or something. I'll make it work."

It probably would work, at least at first. And then the demands of the show and Hunter's endless push for expansion would take over and he'd be looking at just a different version of all the reasons he was leaving. His future, his life with Sophie, crystalized down to a single, immovable word. "No."

Hunter pointed at him. "She's messed you up. You don't even see how much she's messed you up. There's a file saved on my computer showing everything she couldn't get around to telling you. I'm not sure why I even bothered finding out the truth for you, seeing how you're happily stabbing me in the back here. I've emailed it to you—you should take a look. It's fascinating reading. But from here on in, you're on your own. Save yourself, little brother, I'm done trying."

With that, Hunter grabbed his suitcase and

briefcase out of the SUV and began walking back toward the airport.

"Hunter!" Cooper called, even though he knew how pointless it was.

The Pine Brothers were finished.

A pair of tiny, perfect faces poked out from hospital blankets—one pink, one blue. The one-day-old members of the Buckton family filled Tess's heart with joy and wonder.

Ellie was asleep in her room, catching what Gran jokingly called "the last decent sleep she'd get in ages," but her husband, Nash, was accepting congratulations from all the family members who'd gathered to see the twins. Like many lawmen, Ellie's sheriff husband was usually a quieter sort, but not today. Today he beamed with pride and grinned like a fool.

"Sheriff Dad," Luke joked as he elbowed his brother-in-law. "Fine pair of kiddos you got yourself there."

Nash put his hand up to the glass that showed a dozen crying babies while Natalie and Nathan slept peacefully.

"I haven't seen them awake," Luke asked, "what color are the eyes?"

Ruby gave him a look. "It's too early to tell that."

"Maybe not," Gran said. "I've seen enough Buckton babies to know what the color looks like before it comes in." She beamed. "These babies got 'em." She winked at Nash. "You never had a chance."

"Are you kidding?" Nash teased back. "Don't think I don't know these babies had certain…expectations to fill. I've been praying my dark eyes didn't get the best of that Buckton blue trait ever since we knew they were coming." Nash, who bore his Japanese mother's coloring, stared in awe at his daughter and son. "And look at them, they're perfect."

Tess felt mostly happiness, but accepted the twinge of sadness her sudden maternal urges lent to the occasion. *I'll be a mother someday, won't I, Lord? All this affection didn't rise up out of nowhere only to have nowhere to go? Help me trust Your timing and Your plan. I want my heart to be filled only with love for these little ones, not envy or regret over what You've decided I can't yet have.*

Luke walked up beside her. "Get a load of our godchildren. The next Buckton twins to take on the world."

Given Luke's renegade past, Tess could only be astonished at the change in her twin brother. Gran had said leaving the circuit behind and finally settling down with Ruby— who had been the love of his life in high school but been left behind while Luke took on the rodeo world—had changed Luke, and she was right.

"Get a load of my twin brother, cooing at babies," she teased. "And their last name is Larson, remember."

"Maybe, but they're Bucktons all the same. I can see it in their faces."

Tess laughed. "They're asleep. They're one day old. You can't see anything in those faces except cuteness."

Luke pressed his nose up against the glass. "But it's a Buckton brand of cuteness, I can tell." He cast a glance at Tess. "Takes the pressure off us, at least."

Tess startled a bit at his remark. Did he know? "What?"

"Twins. Folks told me it skipped a generation lots of times. I wanted Gran to get another set of twins to coddle, but I don't think I'm up to the challenge of two at once. I mean, I know what we were like."

Gran had often said that even after her own boys, not to mention Gunner and Ellie, Luke and Tess had just about done her in. "So you really are thinking about kids once you and Ruby are married?"

Luke flashed the high-voltage smile that had won him countless female fans in his rodeo days. "I know. Who'd have thunk it?"

Tess managed a laugh. "Wonders never cease."

Luke pushed his hands into his pockets. "Now there's only you to match off. And Cooper Pine sure seems eager for the job the way you are spending time together. I'm surprised you don't know his five-year plan for world domination by now."

She swatted his shoulder, not entirely in jest. "Stop it."

"Well, come on. You spend more time over there than you do on the Blue Thorn. I mean the kid's cute and all, but it's clear you've become a very exclusive member of the Piney brigade."

She hated the idea of being lumped in with those rampant fans with their T-shirts and autograph lines. "He's a friend, Luke. I'm not starstruck." She started to say, "We've never discussed the show," but that would be a lie. The truth was she knew a lot about Cooper's plans after his revelation earlier. She valued his trust and was glad he'd told her, but...the more unsettling truth was that his exit from the Pine Brothers' media to take up this new venture of service had deepened her attraction to the man.

Luke picked up on how she bit her tongue. "Hey, wait, you know something, don't you? I could always tell when you were hiding something. You've been hiding something since you came back—don't even bother denying it."

There really wasn't any point in denying the last part of his statement. Tess was actually surprised Luke hadn't tried to pry things out of her before now. Maybe the fact that she was hiding two different things could buy her some time before sharing her secret. "Not here, okay? This is about Nash and Ellie and their babies."

The nurse gave some kind of signal to Nash, and he walked over to Tess to interrupt her conversation with Luke just in time. "It's almost feeding time for them. Ellie wanted me to get a shot of you and Luke holding Natalie and Nathan—the twins holding the twins, you know?"

"We can hold them?" Luke said, looking far more excited than Tess would have ever guessed.

"I insist. You'll have to gown up, but I think you can handle a yellow paper dress, can't you, cowboy?"

Tess's heart swelled at the thought of holding her little niece. It was part of why she'd come halfway around the world, wasn't it?

Little Natalie's tiny yawn was about as perfect a joy as Tess could imagine as she held the newborn in her arms. Ellie had come home to the Blue Thorn in the midst of her own mess—fleeing a broken engagement with an egotistical jerk who'd cheated on her with her best friend. She certainly hadn't been looking for any more romance, and yet she'd found the love of her life in Nash Larson. And now her sister and her sheriff husband were a family, the parents of two beautiful babies. *I'm looking right at the joy You bring out of strife, Lord. I want to believe You've got joy waiting for me, that the way Bardo and Sophie tug at my heart isn't a misstep or punishment.*

Natalie's tiny, chubby fingers stretched out in a wobbly reach, finding Tess's thumb and grasping on. Tess felt as if God was sending her a hang-on message, a promise that her endurance through this mess would result in great joy. The fact that she and Luke, who had reconnected after a long stretch of silence, could stand there and hold their niece and nephew together as brother and sister— that in itself was cause for praise. *Don't let me forget this*, Tess prayed as she stood next to Luke and grinned for the camera with Natalie's tiny fingers wrapped around her thumb.

Tess nodded over to her handbag in the corner of the ward. "Can you get a shot for me with my phone?" she asked Nash. She wanted to send the picture to Sophie on the new cell phone she'd gotten from her uncle for her birthday—another cute shot to go along with the endless stream of kitten and doll photos. Already on her own phone was an adorable selfie Sophie had taken with Rainbow Sparkle and Molly, the six-year-old's grin as joy-producing to Tess as the yawns of the newborns.

Just as Nash said, "Got it," and tucked her cell phone back into her handbag, Nathaniel began to squall. Natalie started in Tess's arms then began crying herself, followed by more than a few other babies in the nursery. "Feeding time at the zoo," Nash quipped, wincing as his son and daughter launched into full-out wails. "Party's over."

With a little help from the nurse, Nash maneuvered both babies into his arms, an absurdly victorious smile sweeping his features at the accomplishment.

"Will you look at that?" Luke cajoled. "He's a pro already."

"Might as well learn quick," Nash said as they all walked out of the nursery. "We'll be home before you know it."

"And we'll all be waiting to help you," Gran said, patting the little pink hat on Natalie's head—hand knit by Ellie herself, of course—as Nash walked by with the twins. She followed Nash in the direction of Ellie's room. "See you all at home. I'm staying here until Gunner and Audie come by and then he'll bring me home."

Tess waved goodbye to Gran and the tiny new arrivals. They were so all happy. She just had to believe that there was a personal, special happiness out there somewhere waiting for her, too.

"Let's head out," Luke said, stripping off the paper gown.

Tess did the same, reaching for her purse to view the photos. She'd set her phone on vibrate so as not to disturb anyone in the hospital.

Her screen showed two missed phone calls and two texts—all from Cooper. Something was up.

# Chapter Thirteen

When Luke pulled his truck up to the Blue Thorn gate, Tess saw Cooper's SUV sitting on the side of the road. Cooper stood leaning up against one side, wearing an expression she'd never seen on him. He'd often been guarded and, on occasion, he'd been charming. When pressed by her family, she'd seen edges of aggravation and frustration, but never the dark and searing look that dropped her stomach as Luke stopped the car.

"Somebody wants a few words with you," Luke said. "And it doesn't look like they'll be happy ones." Tess had read the text messages saying Cooper wanted to talk to her, and it had sounded urgent, so she'd texted him to say where she was and that she was on her way back to the ranch. She'd suspected he might come over to talk to her, but she hadn't expected the black storm his eyes held right now.

She slipped her cell phone into the pocket of her jeans and opened the truck door. "I'll catch up with you later."

Luke grabbed her hand. "Hey, is everything okay? You want me to stay while you see what Grumps over there is ticked about?"

The gesture of protection—something Luke had always done back before they lost their way with each other—left a warm spot in Tess's heart despite the rising anxiety. "I'll be fine," she said, squeezing his hand. "I'll call you if I need you, but I don't think I will. Only," she added, glancing toward Cooper's razor-sharp stance, "I think this might take a while."

"You sure?" Luke asked, looking a bit worried.

"I'm sure."

She got out of the truck and walked slowly toward Cooper, practically feeling the air prickle as she did.

He stared at her for a moment, eyes sharp and assessing. "What are you doing?" he said slowly.

"I just came back from seeing the twins, like I said in my text. Cooper, what's wrong? What happened? Is Sophie okay?"

"Do you really care about what happens to her? I mean, really?"

What kind of a question was that? "I adore Sophie, you know that. Cooper, what's going on?"

"*Do* you adore her? Or is she just a means to an end? Because if you're using her, so help me—"

"What's this all about?" She cut him off. "I'm not using Sophie for anything. I wouldn't do that. What on earth would I use her for?"

He straightened, and Tess was suddenly reminded of the sheer size of the man. "To get to me. To get to a nice comfy life as my wife that will let you pay off all the money you owe some sleazeball named Jasper Garvey in Adelaide."

Tess fell back against the SUV as if the declaration slammed her there. Her throat closed up in shock, blocking anything close to an explanation. It was hard to breathe, much less defend herself.

"I know about all of it. Or, more precisely, Hunter knows about all of it. Sophie told him everything—and I do mean everything—on the phone yesterday. All about you, and the doll you'd bought her, and the little boy you wanted to adopt in Australia. Hunter grew suspicious of your generosity and did a little digging." He shifted his weight, but in his current state it looked more like a predatory stalk. "For someone asking me to come clean with my own plans, you sure were holding out enough secrets of your own."

Her lungs felt like they were filled with boiling water. He knew. Hunter knew. People she didn't know now knew the things she couldn't even bear to tell Gran. The raw sensation of feeling exposed was overwhelming, making her want to curl in on herself. To run and hide. "I told you I was working through some things." She tried to say it as calmly as she could, but it ended up sounding like gulps instead of words. "Things I was ashamed of. I made mistakes in Adelaide, yes."

"Were you hoping I can fix them? Or at least throw money at them? Deep pockets fix lots of things in this world, or so folks think."

"No." It came out more of a pitiful moan than a word. "No," she tried to repeat more forcefully.

"I told Hunter he was off the mark. Is he?" For a split second the fury in his eyes gave way to pain, giving her hope that Cooper didn't want his brother's accusation to be true.

"Yes. I mean…the facts are all true, about Bardo and Jasper and the money, but not what he said about…us." It stung bone-deep to think that Cooper could believe that about her. Then again, how long had they known each other? Hadn't he told her about all the people who seemed to need something from him? She'd seen how wary he was of letting anyone close.

"I'm not *after you*." The words tasted sour and cheap. "I couldn't do that to Sophie." The accusation made her sound like Jasper, like some shadowy creature who preyed on the trust of good people. "After what Garvey did to me, I'd rather die than do that to someone I cared about." That revealed she cared about Sophie and Cooper, but the confession hardly mattered in light of the circumstances.

Cooper's stance softened the slightest bit. "What did he do? I want to hear it from you."

She was going to have to admit the whole thing to him. Depending on how much Hunter had told him, he might know most of it already, but that didn't make the prospect any less painful or humiliating. "It's a long story."

Cooper walked over and sat on the back bumper of the SUV. "I think you owe me all of it."

She sat on the other side, her stomach roiling. "I did shots for a human interest piece on the foster care system in Adelaide. A magazine article about how well it works, that sort of thing. There was this boy." She closed her eyes, picturing the sweet smile Bardo had always offered her. "I can't explain it. I loved him. I knew he loved me. He fit into this hole in my life I didn't even realize was there. I kept having to go back there—at first to do more work on the piece, then just because I couldn't stop going. The way Gunner describes what it was like to see Trey when he was first born? Well, that's how I felt about Bardo. He was four. I was a twenty-five-year-old, single, American woman. Even attempting to become his mother made no logical sense, but none of the facts mattered. I just couldn't stop…needing him and believing he needed me."

She ran her hands through her hair, striving for the words that would make the whole nonsensical thing make any kind of sense. "I would have done anything they asked. I would have moved there, taken classes, become a citizen, whatever." She ventured a look up at Cooper. "I knew, like I've never known anything about my life, that I'd be incomplete without him. That I *am* incomplete without him." She sighed, suddenly weary.

"So you tried to adopt him." Cooper had every right to look skeptical. "That's a million-to-one shot in Australia—didn't you know that?"

"I knew—or I thought I knew—what a long shot that was. I spent a lot of time trying to figure out ways to convince myself not to try—I mean, really, what young single woman tries to adopt a special needs boy in Australia? But I couldn't let go of the idea, no matter how hard I prayed over it. I convinced myself that it wasn't impossible, not if God wanted it for me." A tight and desperate laugh escaped from her. "And then I met Jasper."

"Jasper Garvey. The guy has a criminal record, Tess."

"I should have checked, I know that. But he found me at just the right moment and told me all the things I wanted to hear. He told me I was so brave to try," Tess went on. "He assured me he could help if I was willing to get 'creative.' He told me a lot of other things that seemed plausible—or maybe they just sounded that way because I was desperate to believe him. He said—" she gave Cooper a helpless look "—just what you just said. That a lot of problems can be solved in this world if you're willing to throw enough money at them. So I was willing to, as he said, 'invest' in making my dream come true." She looked away, not wanting to see the judgment in Cooper's eyes. "I was blind. And stupid."

Tess pushed off the bumper to walk across the latticework of shadows the fence posts threw across the roadside. "I really thought God sent me to Bardo." She hugged her chest, the shame of telling it all still making her whole self feel burned and tender. "That finding Bardo was the point in all my traveling, the destination God wanted me to reach, the tipping point of that great, happy life everyone else seems to have gotten." She turned and looked at Cooper. "Everyone else in my family has had these awesome, long-shot happy endings that came to them just when happiness seemed most out of reach— couldn't it be my turn?"

She waited for him to say something, to give her any indication that she'd defended herself against whatever accusations Hunter had thrown at her. He didn't speak. He wasn't there to speak, she realized. He was there to hear her out. She was grateful he was allowing her that chance, even if his eyes were still more angry than empathetic. She discovered it was hard, but not unbearable, to pull the story out of the dark place where it had festered in her heart.

"I used all the money I had, and then some,

because I believed Jasper when he'd said funds donated to the right places could speed my way into the system. He promised me it wasn't illegal. He promised me I wasn't doing anything that amounted to 'buying' Bardo. I need you to believe me that I felt I was going the extra mile, not falling for a trap or doing anything underhanded."

Cooper watched Tess pause and wait. He knew she wanted to hear him say he believed her, but the washed-out feeling that had swallowed him ever since Hunter had shared his revelation wouldn't let him. He was accustomed to his skill at reading people. Those he let close never shocked and betrayed him like this. Tess had withheld a mountain of information from him and he'd allowed it, allowed her into his and Sophie's lives because she'd appealed to some long shut-down part of him. He couldn't shake the notion that she'd tricked him just as easily as this Jasper bloke had tricked her. And that stung.

"I got taken," she declared as if she'd read his thoughts in his eyes. "I can see that clear as day—now—but I was blinded back then. I have no one to blame but me." She sat back down on the bumper and part of him felt how close she was while another part of him tensed at the proximity. "I'm smarter than this—or maybe I'm not, I don't know anymore." Defeat weighted her words. He'd thought just the same thing, and hearing his own feelings and fears spoken in her voice tangled his composure.

She turned to him. The lost look in her eyes seeped through his defenses no matter what shield he raised. "I only know I crawled home in debt up to here—" she thrust her hand above her head "—and feeling like I wasn't worth anything to anyone—that there wasn't a single thing I could do right. Until your daughter took a liking to me."

He knew Sophie could do that to people. He also knew Sophie trusted anyone, which meant she could trust the wrong people. It was her greatest gift and his deepest worry, the reason he protected her so fiercely.

Tess's eyes brimmed with tears. "She made me feel better about myself. As if I might be capable of *one shred of good* despite all the stupid things I'd done."

His arms felt like they were straining to reach for her even as he stood stock-still. She hasn't explained everything, he reminded himself. Everything she said could be true—and likely was—but didn't discount Hunter's accusation. Even if her reasons for getting into debt were innocent…the debt was still there. What was she going to do about it? Was she hoping to get financial help from him? Desperate people did desperate things. There were questions he needed to ask, but half of him feared the answers. It struck him, as he sat looking at her and tamping down the war going off in his chest, that he wanted Hunter to be wrong.

But wanting it didn't make it true.

He'd wanted—no, needed—Grace to live, but that hadn't happened, either.

He didn't know how to ask what he needed to know. *Are you after my money?* Even if he was willing to believe she sincerely cared for him and for Sophie, that didn't necessarily mean the money wasn't a factor. It might not be the only thing she liked about him, but it could still play into the way she'd tried to connect to his family. He was asking for something nearly impossible to prove: her intentions. Even for someone with all his perceptive skills, how could he ever really know a person's heart in something as complicated as this?

"Say something." Tess was crying now, and not even trying to stop. It was heartbreaking to watch, and he waited to feel something, anything, that would give him a clue as to how to react. It was as if all the conflicting impulses—to comfort her or to push her away—canceled each other out, leaving him feeling nothing.

"What do you want from me?" he asked.

Her eyes flashed at his question, hard and shiny with tears and pain. "I don't want your money, Cooper, if that's what you're worried about. You can tell your snooping brother to call off his dogs. Half of the debt I was able to take care of by selling just about everything I have. As for the rest… I've already asked Gran for help, and that was awful enough, believe me. I'd much rather do this on my own, but I can't." She nearly spat out the last two words. "I'm not looking to you to bail me out of this. And, I have to say, it's a low blow that you think me capable of it."

"I'm not sure I do."

She gave a thin, dark laugh. "Well, I suppose I should be flattered you at least have second thoughts about my skills as a gold-digger."

He didn't find that particularly amusing. "Why didn't you tell me?"

"Admit my colossal mistake to a man I've known all of three weeks? Who's keeping a few major secrets of his own?"

She had him there. Only she didn't. "It was more than that."

Her body reacted with a kind of startled softness and he knew she understood his meaning. Even though it had only been a few weeks, they were closer than they ought to be, bonded in ways that never paid much attention to timetables. That was half the problem—in many ways he'd come to care for a stranger.

"Is Hunter wrong?" It seemed the only question truly worth asking.

Her sigh deflated her against the back of the SUV. "About my mess of a life? No. I did all those things. I'm in hot water financially. I'm a basket case emotionally. I don't think I'm washed up professionally, but I'm probably pretty close. I didn't tell you any of it, which might not have been fair. I went way overboard with Sophie, I get that. But it felt so good to make her happy.

"It's like I was starving for that, had it taken from me with Bardo, and I couldn't stop doing anything and everything I could think of to have a chance to affect a child in a positive way—to make things better the way I wanted to before." She turned her head to face him. "Hunter is wrong. I have not played you. I—" she raised her fingers in the air and wiggled them "—like you too much."

There could not have been a less appropriate time to invoke "air quotes" or his own overheard words to Glenno. The way she was bumbling her way through this relationship—and he dreaded to even use that word in these circumstances—both irritated and endeared him. He'd always had a thing for lost souls. And right now, both of them were a little too lost.

"I told you everything," he said. "Not at first, but I told you. If I hadn't confronted you today, would you ever have told me?"

"Do you know how many times I almost did? It would be like ripping my heart out and handing it to you to stomp on, but part of me wanted to see if you *would* stomp. Most of me hoped you would help me figure out some way to put the pieces back together. Not with money. I'll say that as many times as you need to hear it—I was never after your money. But you're Cooper Pine. People make mistakes with their horses all the time and you fix them." She started crying again. "I suppose I wanted you to fix me. But not in the way Hunter thinks. Never in the way Hunter thinks."

They sat in silence, the sun throwing longer shadows across the fields. Tess sniffed, and Cooper reached into his pocket and handed her his handkerchief. He was careful to keep their fingers from touching when he did, and she noticed.

"Do you believe me?" Her words were so fragile.

He'd known and depended on Hunter his whole life. He'd known Tess less than a month. "I want to."

She exhaled. "Not the same, is it?"

A cheery, silly song chirped from the open window of the SUV. "Sophie," he said, almost glad of the distraction. "Hunter showed her how to make her own ringtone on my phone."

Tess wiped her eyes and straightened her hair. "Sounds exactly like her."

Cooper nabbed the phone, lit up with a goofy picture of Sophie—another of Hunter's ideas—and hit the button to accept the call. "Hi, sunshine," he said, forcing a normal tone into his words.

"Where are you? It's almost suppertime and Glenno made meat loaf."

"I'm almost home. I'm talking to Miss Tess for a moment." He tried never to lie to Sophie, and he didn't have enough wits about him now to start.

"Oooh!" she cooed. "Can she come to supper? Can you ask her?"

Tess, who had walked over, put her hand to her forehead as she heard the question. Cooper caught her gaze as he answered, "Not tonight, baby. I'll be home in a few minutes, okay?"

"Okay. Tell Miss Tess that Rainbow Sparkle is being a good little kitty."

Tess clearly heard, but he answered. "I will. Now go wash up for supper and I'll be there."

"Yep." Sophie ended the call, and Cooper stood there with the phone in his hand, at a loss for how to end this conversation.

Tess beat him to it. "You have to go." There was an awful resignation to her words, as if she was sure she'd now have to add her friendship with him and Sophie to her pile of mistakes.

"I do." She flinched a bit at the words and he felt it twist and cut inside. "Look, I don't know what's next here. Things are messed up and I need to be careful. I need..." What did he need? He wasn't sure, and that scared him. "Some time, I reckon." He didn't know how much, or why, he only knew too much had been thrown at him in the last twenty-four hours to think straight.

"Okay," she said softly, resignation in her eyes.

"I want to believe you." He owed her that reassurance.

"You can, you know." She backed up a bit and he felt the distance pull at him. "Or you can decide you don't. You know it all now. I've got nothing left to lose."

Tess turned and punched the entry code into the Blue Thorn Ranch gate. It struck him, as he watched her slow, slumped walk up the drive, that he perhaps had a great deal to lose here.

# Chapter Fourteen

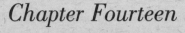

"God bless Mommy in Heaven and Uncle Hunter and Glenno and Rainbow Sparkle and the two new babies in Audie's family." Sophie's eyes squinted shut in adorably fervent prayer. "God bless Miss Tess and the people who made Molly and everyone at my new church. Amen."

Sophie's list of "God blesses" never ceased to be one of the highlights of Cooper's day. She had such a big heart for a soul that had taken so many hits in her young life. *Thank You for her,* Cooper prayed as he sat on the end of her bed. *I couldn't have made it without her. I want to help all the kids just like her with this ranch.*

"Daddy," Sophie said with a serious tone, "I've decided something."

Cooper took the stack of books from off

her blanket and set them on the nightstand. "Have you now? What's that?"

"I really do want a new leg."

"Well, you can certainly have one if that's what you want." Molly was tucked in bed beside Sophie, and out of the corner of his eye Cooper saw the doll's prosthetic standing in the closet beside Sophie's. Even though he was pretty sure he knew the answer, he asked anyway. "Why now all of a sudden? Molly?"

"Sort of. I mean, I want to be able to carry her and Rainbow Sparkle and everything, so that's part of it. Mostly, I figure if I have a new church and a new home and I'm getting a new mom, I should have a new leg, right?"

Cooper sat straight. "Sweetheart, I thought we talked about this. Is that what you told Uncle Hunter about Miss Tess?" He hadn't yet found a way to bring up yesterday's troublesome phone call with Hunter—maybe this was his opening.

"I told him I thought Miss Tess should be my new mommy." Sophie said it with such a happy acceptance that Cooper had no idea how to respond. She caught his expression, furrowing her little strawberry-blond brows. "You told Glenno you liked her. She told me she likes you. She gave me Rainbow Sparkle and Molly."

Cooper fumbled for a reply. "Miss Tess is very nice. And I know she's taken quite a shine to you. I know you like Molly and Sparkle a whole lot. But like I said before, a new mommy is…well, it's a great big deal."

"Miss Tess says it's—" Sophie made a face getting the big word out "—complicated."

Cooper wanted to go into all the reasons why that was true, but he decided instead to ask a more important question. "Are you sure you're ready for a new mommy? Aren't you happy with me?"

"You're sad. Uncle Hunter says you're lonely. Glenno says you're thinking hard."

Some days Sophie's perception stunned him. "Those are what other people say. What do you say?"

"I think Mommy would like the way Miss Tess and I are friends."

"You can be friends with Miss Tess without her being your mommy." Of course, given the conversation out by the gate, Cooper wasn't sure that was true anymore. Would he be comfortable having Tess around Sophie after the day's revelations? And if Tess continued to spend time with Sophie, what would it mean for her relationship with him? Would they be able to take a step back from the feelings growing between them?

Whatever it was between him and Tess, it wouldn't ever fit into the confines of friendship. He'd become doubly aware of his attraction to Tess since his argument with Hunter. In fact, he'd thought of nothing else. "We're here so you can have lots of new friends, not just Miss Tess and Audie."

"I know, and I like the kids I've met so far. I like Audie lots. But I like how Miss Tess looks at you. She smiles when you smile, and you smile when she does."

"She's been very nice to us. But that doesn't mean she should be your new mommy." Questioning Tess's motives bothered him deeply. He was steamed at the prospect of being played, as Hunter put it. But the thought of being played by Tess Buckton seemed devastating and impossible.

But was it? If she truly was manipulating him as Hunter accused, that'd be the end of her in his life and Sophie's. He didn't want that. He wanted Tess in his life very much, and that perception could easily cloud his thinking. He thought of what Tess had said about how she'd been blind to Jasper's manipulations because she'd wanted so badly to believe him. Was Cooper falling into the same trap?

"I asked God," Sophie said, pulling Cooper from his thoughts.

"What did you ask Him?" Pride at her pint-size prayer life warred with worry over what answer she believed she got.

"I asked Him if Tess was my new mommy. I told Him I thought she'd be a good one, and that she made you happy."

Cooper made a show of peering at his daughter. "How old are you again?"

She giggled. "You know I'm six."

"Oh, for a minute there I thought maybe you were sixteen, asking God such big, grown-up questions and telling Him who makes me happy."

"Well, she does. Even Glenno says he can see it. I heard him telling Uncle Hunter about it on his own phone."

So Hunter had polled Glenno about the situation, as well, had he? "What did you hear when you said that prayer?"

"Nothing, really. No one really hears God, Daddy."

Cooper disagreed. He'd argue to his final breath that God had quite clearly told him Pine Purpose Ranch was to be his next life's work. "I hear God all the time, sunshine."

Sophie looked incredulous. "Not in words."

"Well, no, not in words like you and I

use—we've talked about this. But you can hear God in feelings and people and things coming together and things coming into and out of your life."

"Like Miss Tess coming into ours. I feel happy when I think about it. That supposed-to-be feeling you always tell me about. That's the answer I got. About her and Rainbow Sparkle, and Molly, and now my leg."

Cooper began to feel he was losing this particular debate. "Sometimes people do things to make you feel like they're a supposed-to-be when they're not." It was the closest he could come to explaining what Tess might possibly have done. He'd never mentioned the issue with Lynette because he didn't want to taint Sophie's view of the world. Maybe that had been a mistake. "It's sad to see, but some people are nice to you because they want something from you, not because they really like you."

"Oh, I know. I've seen Uncle Hunter be nice to people and then turn around and frown when they aren't looking."

Hunter could be a bit disingenuous, but that wasn't the same thing. How could he explain this to someone Sophie's age? "I think you should be nice to everyone, but I also think it's smart to think carefully about who you trust. Especially when you do something lots of people know about and want to be around, like what I do with the Pine Method." *Did.* As much as he felt sure of the decision, referring to the Pine Method in the past tense was going to take some getting used to.

"I think the new ranch will be really special," Sophie said, yawning. "I think I'll make lots of friends. And I'm glad you'll be home lots more."

It warmed his heart to hear her put his wishes in her own words. "Me, too, sunshine. But it might have to be okay if Miss Tess isn't part of that."

"Nooooo," Sophie whined, her eyes popping back open. "She has to be. Why can't she be?"

*Because I have to think carefully about who we can trust*, Cooper told himself. "Because Miss Tess and I had a very big fight." It was the only way he could think of to describe it.

"Then you need to fix it with her like you always tell me to do. You gotta, Daddy."

Cooper sighed. "Some grown-up fights don't have fixes. Don't worry, I'm sure you'll still have Audie as a friend no matter what. I'm just not sure Miss Tess and I can be friends."

"Because you like her too much?"

For as confused as Sophie looked, she'd declared the true issue. "Grown-ups can be goofy that way. I don't expect you to understand, but you might when you get older."

"I don't think so."

"Let's leave that problem for tomorrow, okay? We'll both sleep on it and talk some more in the morning."

"Okay."

Cooper kissed his daughter good-night but doubted he'd be getting much sleep at all tonight. He felt far too unsettled to close his eyes anytime soon.

Gran pushed the door open to Tess's room the next morning.

Tess had gone straight into her room after that awful conversation with Cooper and had not emerged since.

Gran's bathrobe was soft and butter-yellow, sunny like the woman who wore it. Gran was one of those endlessly optimistic people who could say that things would look better in the morning and truly mean it. She'd seen enough loss and estrangement in her life—Grandpa's passing, Mom dying when Tess was only eleven, Dad's slow and sour exit from life—to make her a bitter old woman, but not Gran. *How do I get that? How do I crawl up from the hole I'm in?* Tess asked God as she patted her bed for Gran to come sit beside her.

Gran folded her hands in her lap as she sat. "You didn't come down for pancakes."

Tess loved Gran's pancakes—they were the favorite comfort or celebration food of all the Buckton children. "I wasn't hungry this morning." Nor could she stomach all the new-baby happiness that would fill the table alongside the family members.

"Luke told me he dropped you off at the gate to talk with Cooper Pine yesterday afternoon after the hospital. He told me Cooper looked as if he'd swallowed an angry snake."

It was a fair—if creative—description. She'd never seen Cooper angry before and hoped to never see it again. She simply nodded, sitting up against the headboard, feeling like a kid staying home sick from school.

"Does whatever is going on between you two have to do with this trouble you're in?" Gran asked.

Tess felt like slumping down and pulling the blankets over her head. "Yes and no. It doesn't, but Cooper's brother thinks it does, that I'm trying to..." She simply moaned. "Oh, does it even matter?"

Gran got that look on her face—the don't-mess-with-me look all the Bucktons feared.

Gran had the longest fuse of anyone she'd ever met, but when you got to the end of it, look out. "I think it's time you tell me what's going on. All of it."

Tess felt too washed-out to care how bad things looked. Hunter's accusations, delivered via Cooper, had dragged it out of her last night, what did it matter if she spilled it all out again this morning?

She told the whole story—Bardo, Jasper, the money, the failed adoption attempt, Sophie—all of it, ending with Hunter's suspicions and Cooper's doubts. There were no tears this time, the pain and shame had been replaced by a vague, numb resignation.

"Why, child?" Gran patted Tess's leg. "Why couldn't you tell me? Or Luke? Or someone? I feel like I've been watching you waste away while you've been here." She reached for Tess's hand and shook it. "Home is where you can come with something that hurts this bad. It's the whole point of family."

Tess pulled her knees up to hug them. "Parade my huge mistake in front of all my happy brothers and sisters with their nice, shiny, new lives? Who could resist?"

"Luke would swat you if he heard you talk like that. He limped home—literally, after falling off that bull—in worse shape than you. And he did some dumb things before Ruby knocked some sense into him, mind you. All your brothers and sisters fought hard for those happy endings. Only, you talk like you've got no fight left in you. What that Jasper fellow did to you was a crime. Why aren't you fighting back? Pressing charges?"

She had thought about it. Early on, before it had become apparent how foolish she'd been not doing research, swallowing the bait Jasper had so cleverly laid out in front of her. "Then everyone would know."

Gran sat back. "I hate to burst your bubble, hon, but sounds like word's out, anyway. I'd think less of you for letting this varmint walk away clean than I do for going too far in trying to make a life with someone you love." She looked at Tess. "You love that little boy. I can see that, plain as day. You thought you were giving all you had to bring the two of you together. That isn't wrong—it's what Jasper did that's wrong. Don't you think for one minute otherwise."

"But Cooper and Sophie…"

"Well, that's a whole other thing, those two. Not that nonsense about you being after his money—I know there's not a lick of truth to that. But there may be something to the idea that you're trying to fill that hole in your life with them. You've got to decide how you feel about them and whether it's real or just a stand-in for little Bardo. Love's got to go somewhere when it gets all fired up like that, and sometimes it finds the wrong place if it can't have the right one."

Tess moaned. "How am I supposed to know that?"

"Well, it's nothing I can tell you, that's for sure. What's your heart tell you?"

"That the timing's all off and the circumstances couldn't be worse."

Gran tapped Tess on the forehead. "That's your brain yapping, sugar. Tell me what your heart says. Close your eyes, think of that man and his little girl, and tell me what you feel."

"Gran…"

Gran replied with a do-as-you're-told look Tess knew better than to ignore. Gran might be small and well on in her years, but the woman could be relentless when she chose to be. Tess closed her eyes and thought about Sophie touching the doll, and Cooper's expression as he'd caught her eyes over Sophie's head. How, right then, for the first time since everything had unraveled, she'd felt right. Worth something in this world. Capable of doing good and feeling like she belonged.

"Well, that's that," Gran said before Tess even opened her eyes.

"Huh?" Tess peered at her grandmother.

"Sweetheart." Gran crossed her arms over her chest. "You can say any words you want, but I saw it written all over your face, clear as day. The old Tess, the one ready to take on the world, she came back just now. With a big, old, warm glow besides. You care for Cooper, and near as I can tell, he cares for you."

"It doesn't matter now."

Gran uncrossed her arms. "It matters now more than ever!"

"I don't know if he believes me."

"So convince him. Sophie believes in you. Sophie adores you. And, goodness, the man's plans couldn't make me happier. I'd donate toward his therapy ranch right this minute if I could. We were wrong about him, thinking he'd bring trouble or chaos here. I'll own up to it when the time comes, but first thing is to prove to him his brother's wrong about you. Now, how are you gonna do that?"

"I don't know." Tess wished her voice didn't sound so whiny, but she truly was stumped.

"Well, you're not gonna find out sitting up here sulking. And it'll be awkward to draw up a loan payment schedule with the accountant while we're still in our jammies."

"You can loan me the money?"

"Not all of it. We'll have to come up with some other solution for the last bit, but I can get you started." She paused before she added, "It might help to bring your brothers and sisters in on this. Swallow your pride, hon. This situation is not the black mark you're making it. We've all made our share of mistakes, and we won't judge you for yours. Helping each other out is the whole point of family."

"It'll kill me to tell them," Tess replied, already picturing the look Gunner would give her for being taken in by the likes of Jasper.

"Nonsense. You just told me, and you look alive and well on account of it. Well, alive at least. You'll look more well once we get you out of those pj's. We love you. I'm thinking you just might love Cooper. God can take care of the rest—but only if you get out of bed."

Tess looked up at her grandmother. There really was only love in her eyes, not judgment or pity or disappointment or any of the other things she feared. "I love you, Gran."

Gran kissed Tess's forehead, the way she'd always done when Tess was a little girl. "That's my girl. Mercy, but it's good to see you back on the Blue Thorn. I'm so very glad you came on home."

*Me, too*, Tess thought. And for the first time since she boarded that international flight, it didn't feel like a defeat to be home. It felt like it just might be a new beginning.

## Chapter Fifteen

Cooper didn't sleep. The morning rose bleary and troublesome, his whole body and soul feeling sore, tired and out of sorts. He was just finishing feeding the last horse when he looked up to see a blue truck sitting outside the ranch gate.

Tess. He wasn't ready for this.

Still, they couldn't ignore each other forever. Not when they were living less than a mile apart. So even though he still had no idea what to do about the whole situation, Cooper found himself walking toward the gate.

She got out of the truck and waited when she saw him coming toward her, leaning nervously against the hood of the vehicle.

He leaned up against the gate, not sure if

he should open it. "No one buzz you in up at the house?"

"I've been sitting here trying to decide if I should hit that little red button at all. Whether you would even talk to me."

He didn't like to think of himself as that harsh. Cooper held her eyes for a moment before hitting the button that rolled the gate aside. He walked out to her, because that felt safer than letting her in. The look on her face from the last time they talked had burned itself into his brain, showing up every time he closed his eyes. He was wavering already and that was bad.

"I'll talk to you," he said slowly. "But I'll be straight—I'm not sure I know what to say."

In contrast, she looked like she had plenty say. "Do you believe me?"

That really was the crux of it all, wasn't it? "Before we get to that, there's something you should know."

The day was beautiful—the kind of clear, sunny afternoon that had made him fall in love with the ranch in the first place—and he stood looking out over the land. Initially, he'd thought buying this place a sensible idea. In the time he'd been here, the land had dug into his heart. He really did feel as if the ranch had been sitting there waiting for him. As if he was the only man who could turn the land into what it was meant to be.

Cooper leaned up against the stone pillars that formed the gate. For a split second his mind overlaid the "PP" Pine Purpose logo and brand that he had gotten drawn up, and he could imagine seeing the interlaced letters affixed to the rocks, their rustic copper standing out against the stone.

"Earlier this year," he began, "I got into a long mess with one of the production staff from the show. She—" he watched Tess's eyes register the pronoun and its implications "—was a strong member of our staff, and very pretty. She paid a lot of attention to me—much more than the job required. Hunter liked the idea of me going out with her, giving dating another try. And so, for the first time since Grace's passing, I allowed myself to pay attention back."

Tess shifted her weight against the truck but offered no reply.

"I'm very careful about who I let into Sophie's life. At least, I've tried to be. Parts of being famous, doing what I do, are blessings. I get that I have opportunities other people dream about. But that's just the point—there are a lot of people in this world who want something from me."

"I don't want anything from you," Tess said.

"And all of them say exactly that," Cooper replied. "The hardest part about what I do is figuring out who really means it. I'd been pretty good at that up until Lynette. She was a mistake. Things got ugly, and we had to get lawyers involved. The only blessing in the whole mess was that I hadn't gotten Sophie involved."

"I've already told you I'd never hurt Sophie."

"And you need to know I've heard that before, too. I took a chance and told Lynette about Sophie. Lynette acted like that was wonderful, and begged me to meet Sophie, to spend time with her. I let her become one of the few people on the show staff who even knew I had a daughter. Do you have any idea what it feels like to ask a legal team to issue a gag order to someone about your own daughter?"

"Sophie's amazing. Why do you feel you need to hide her from the world?"

She wasn't getting it. "Because of people like Lynette and your Jasper guy who wouldn't think twice about finding some way to use her for their own gain. The last thing I want is someone proposing some docudrama about my life or hers, and believe me, it will happen if the public at large finds out that I have a special needs daughter. I can't even say Hunter wouldn't come up with the idea on his own." He allowed himself a long stare into Tess's eyes. "I won't ever risk Sophie that way. Not ever."

She surprised him by holding his gaze. "You know what I think? I think the person you won't ever risk is you."

He straightened at her accusation. He hadn't expected her to go on the offensive in this, and it startled him.

"I get that you've been hurt. You lost Grace in the worst possible way, and I won't pretend to know what that feels like. Most people probably wouldn't say that I lost Bardo at all because I never truly had him and he's still alive and safe even though he's not with me. And yet I feel like a cannonball went through my chest. It must be a thousand times worse to love someone the way you loved Grace and have her ripped away from you like that, with Sophie's injury making you worry that you might lose her, too."

It was. It was a thousand cannonballs coming at him in all directions, beating him down until it hurt just to breathe, just to still be taking up space on the planet. It tore him to shreds to hold up for Sophie's sake when he wanted to lie down and let the earth swallow him up if that was what it took to stop the pain. He'd traveled from excruciating pain to semi-bearable pain to hollow numbness to the first steps of feeling again when Lynette had pushed everything back to square one. How could he make Tess understand he wouldn't survive another round?

"After I came back from Australia, the first time I felt even close to a functioning human being again was with Sophie," Tess said as she pushed off the truck and began walking toward him.

He felt his spine go rigid, scrambling for a defense he wasn't sure he had.

"I went overboard," she admitted. "I get that. But it was a good overboard. I won't apologize for it because she did something for me that I needed. So, yeah, I need something from you. From her. I need to keep feeling the way I feel when I make her smile or she holds that kitten or that amazing moment when she got a look at that doll." Tess looked straight at him. "Or…or when you take down even a piece of that really high wall you've built around yourself to let me in just a little bit more. You're lonelier than I am, Cooper Pine, and that's saying something."

It hurt—in the closest, most unstoppable

way—to hear her say that about him. He wanted to shout some childish version of "I am not!" but neither of them would believe it. As bad as it was to hear her call him lonely, the worse pain was that it was true. Where did he get off thinking he was hiding it? Even Sophie had picked up on his unhappiness. He knew he should say something but at the moment all he could do was grind his teeth and keep standing there.

Her voice softened and she took another step toward him. "Everyone needs things, Cooper, that's how real life works. Lynette was false and fake, and I hate that there are people like her, like Jasper, in the world. Only now you're letting that woman convince you that there are no true people, no one who can give you the things you need and deserve. I've decided I'm going fight against what Jasper did to me, but you've stopped fighting what Lynette did to you. And whether you like it or not, that's teaching Sophie that life and love are things to be scared of. And that little girl needs to love. Didn't that kitten show you how much love she has to show the world?"

That silly, adorable kitten with the ridiculous name. How was it that a near stranger could do something he'd meant to do for months and make Sophie happier than he had in a long time? Tess was calling him out on a whole bunch of levels, and it felt like his insides were rearranging themselves without his permission. Sophie's ability to love was the greatest wonder of his life, a part of her he never wanted to stifle or suppress. He wanted to say that but only managed to choke out the single word. "Yes."

She gave him one of her looks, the kind that hinted at the fighter she used to be before the whole business with Bardo had knocked the wind out of her sails. "You're gonna have to do better than that." And she stood there, hand on one hip, waiting for him to do just that.

He broke away from her stare, pacing across the roadside. "You scare me," he blurted out, too flustered to care that it sounded as ridiculous as Rainbow Sparkle's name. "I don't know anything about you, or what you want from me, or whether I can trust you." If she wanted honesty, she was going to get it. "I don't seem to be able to stay cautious around you. You're always getting under my skin. And…" He made himself say it, made himself force the words out. "I can't handle how much Sophie likes you."

She took another step toward him. "That's not all of it." She spread her arms, her voice cracking in a way that nearly did him in. "Let's talk about all of it, Cooper."

Tess held her hands wide, ready to risk it all. "I need you. I can't explain it. I'm in the worst possible place to trust the idea of caring for any man, but I need you." She took a deep breath. "Sophie, I get—I see how she fills the hole Bardo left. But you? I don't know how *you* happened." The tears were starting but what did it matter? She was making a fool of herself anyway; crying couldn't really make it any worse. "*Did* you happen? Did 'us' happen? Or did I just make the whole thing up because I needed it on some level?"

She searched his eyes for some crack in the armor, some clue that she wasn't going to walk away from this conversation shut out and humiliated. *Just say you care. Even once. What do I have to confess to get you to open up to me again?* "I'm a mess. I've got problems, but I'm not looking for you to solve them."

"I want to believe you."

He kept saying that. "So believe me."

"Do you have any idea how...how—" he scrunched his face up, hands fisting as he reached in frustration for a word "—invasive you are?"

It was probably a poor move to burst out laughing at his absurd choice of words, but the tension had wound her so tight she couldn't really help herself.

He ran his hands down his face. "Okay, maybe not the best word there."

"No," she said, wiping away tears. "Actually, I think it's pretty accurate. Not entirely complimentary—I think I would have preferred something like 'unforgettable' rather than something that makes me sound like a persistent disease—but I'm not picky."

He looked at her and the crack she'd been waiting for began to show itself. Her entire body lightened as if someone had just cut all the ropes that had been tightening around her for days. "You *are* unforgettable." The air hung still for a moment until he added, "That's the problem."

"Maybe it doesn't have to be a problem."

Cooper gave her a long look. There was longing in his eyes, but a dozen other emotions were in there, too. "I can't afford to make a mistake here," he said.

Panic cut through her earlier relief. He looked so conflicted, she couldn't say if this would be the start of a relationship or their last conversation. Even when the tangle of her pursuit of Bardo had come unraveled, she'd never felt the choking level of vulnerability that covered her now. She couldn't compound the heartbreak of Bardo with the pain of losing Cooper and Sophie. She wouldn't survive. She knew with absolute certainty that if it came to that, she would just stop being.

Tess tried to fight the surge of desperation that came out of nowhere. "I know you can't. And I know I'm nothing but a pile of mistakes right now. Except for you and Sophie. Everything I've shared with the two of you has been the opposite of a mistake. It's right. I know it's right." It took the last ounce of bravery she had to close the distance between them. "Don't you?"

He stiffened. "I want it to be."

That wasn't a yes. It wasn't a no, but it wasn't a yes, either. Her fingers wove themselves together, tight and fretting. "Just tell me I'm not making up the connection between us because I need somebody to care about me. Tell me you feel it." She wanted to beg him, "Tell me you care," but the troubled look in his eyes kept her from going that far.

His pause was excruciating. He was entirely still, except for his chest, which was rising and falling, breathing hard. He was fighting. Even if she'd shut her eyes, Tess was sure the sense of conflict would radiate off him in the prickle she felt down the back of her neck. "I feel it," he said so low and soft she barely heard him.

And then he said, "But…"

For a moment Tess stopped hearing whatever he'd said. The other words didn't matter; the one word had caved everything else in. The roar of her crumbling heart drowned out the whole world.

She wasn't worth the risk. Whatever they could have wasn't worth fighting for. At least to him.

When she pulled herself back to the moment, he was saying something kind about needing time or being unready, but it was all little more than noise—she could barely make out every other word. He looked genuinely sad, and she realized she'd gotten what she'd asked for—his admission that he felt something. She just hadn't realized that his refusal to act on it would hurt worst of all. It would have been better, she realized, if he'd said no.

"Yes, *but…*" was a hundred times worse than no.

"Try to understand," Cooper was saying, his voice tight and strained.

"I get it," she said with a voice that felt as if it came from someone else.

There was an awful, raw moment where

neither of them knew what to say. At this point, what *was* there to say, anyway? The timing was off, he wasn't convinced of her sincerity, and he had every right to be cautious. She couldn't make him take a leap of faith. Somewhere in the back of her brain the mournful song lyric "I can't tell you you love me" lilted, and Tess felt the quietly huge sound of her heart breaking. She didn't know if she loved Cooper Pine, but she'd never know now. Or, if she did know, she'd know it alone.

"Tess…"

Saying her name felt like a knife blade slicing open the thin skin of her life. Everything she'd worked so hard to hold together seemed to have poured out, spilling to the ground to lie useless. Somewhere in the back of her mind there always was the possibility he wouldn't believe her, wouldn't let her further into his life, but she'd worked herself up so much to make this plea that she'd blocked out the prospect of his rejection. And it wasn't even strong enough to be called a rejection. It was a dismissal. A discard. A leaving behind.

A stunned, hollow practicality took over. "Yeah, well, there it is."

"Tess…" he repeated, and the sound of it made her close her eyes against the pain. "I can't give you what you're looking for here. Not yet, at least."

He didn't trust her. There would be no way to prove to him that he could. She knew that now with a pale ring of clarity. Even if clearing the debt on her own would prove it to him, that would take her months—maybe years—even with the help Gran was giving her. And, really, if he couldn't see her heart now, when she'd splayed it out before him like this, what was the point?

She could make some offer about being friends, but they both knew that wasn't an option. Not with Sophie in the picture, so determined to take any opening to push them together. Funny, she'd always thought of Luke as the all-or-nothing twin. But there were no compromises here. Not in this.

She should say goodbye, but she couldn't bring herself to speak the word. And, really, living across the road from each other, it would be silly to think they'd never see each other again. Tess didn't know what was next. She only knew she couldn't survive one more minute of looking at that man as he stood with his eyes on her, the setting sun washing him in gold and shadows.

"I'm sorry," he said, barely getting the

words out. He did feel for her—it was obvious—just not enough.

There weren't words. At least not any she could find. She turned and got back in the truck.

He stood perfectly still as she started the engine and turned around. He hadn't moved when she opened the Blue Thorn gate and floored it up the drive. When she got out of the truck at the top of the rise, she forced herself to look back.

Cooper still stood there, a solitary man casting a long black shadow behind him.

## Chapter Sixteen

The day went downhill from there and hadn't improved one bit the following morning. The world would be a much happier place if it weren't for money, he thought. These days, it wasn't hard to believe it was the root of all evil—or the love of it, he thought the scripture said. He didn't love money lately. He was coming to hate everything it had done to his life. Cooper looked up from the bank's email requesting three more financial documents to find Sophie staring at him with disappointed eyes.

"Why can't I invite Audie and Miss Tess over to play with Rainbow Sparkle? Daddy, why?" Sophie was tugging on his sleeve now. He'd put off telling Sophie about his conversation with Tess, hoping some strategy would come to him, some perfect way to explain this so his daughter would understand. It hadn't.

He pulled Sophie up on his lap as he closed his laptop. "Miss Tess and I had another fight yesterday. A really big one this time."

She frowned. "So go say you're sorry. That's what you always tell me to do."

Rainbow Sparkle bounded into the room. The kitten followed Sophie everywhere and had finagled her way into free run of the house. Cooper didn't much care for the way the little beast acted as if she already owned the place. He certainly didn't care for the way she leaped up onto his desk, and sat on his laptop, as if to say, "Let's see how you get out of this one, cowboy."

"I did say I was sorry, and I *am* sorry we're fighting, but sorry doesn't always fix things. The things we're fighting about can't really change."

Sophie's brow furrowed as she tried to understand. "Can I still be friends with her? And Audie?"

He'd been dreading that question. "I don't know, sunshine. I hope so—especially with Audie. But we may have to wait a bit while everybody gets a chance to feel better." *Feel better. Fat chance of that.* He'd been miserable since he watched that truck turn around and go back up the Blue Thorn drive. He'd spent several long times of prayer begging God to show him what to do, and come away with unnerving silence each time. He'd even called Hunter and told him about their conversation just so he could hear his brother's list of all the reasons why Tess was "bad news not worth the risk."

Hunter made all kinds of sense, in a harsh, business-minded, Hunter kind of way, but nothing he'd said had made Cooper feel any better about his choices. Every time he shut his eyes he saw how the tears ran down Tess's cheeks and how her fingers knotted themselves together in vulnerable agony. The sight of Molly, with her little pink doll crutches and her spiffy pink doll prosthetic, turned his gut to one giant black knot. His head could calculate the risk, but his heart still refused to classify Tess as either bad news or a risk not worth taking.

Tess wasn't Lynette, even if she looked like it on the surface to Hunter. The situation with the production assistant had been much less dangerous. His attraction to Lynette had been lukewarm, the trial run of a heart torn to pieces. What he felt for Tess went far deeper, and that scared him. It made him doubt his ability to see clearly.

"I'm sad," Sophie said.

"I am, too."

His daughter squinted up at him. "What did you mean when you said you liked Miss Tess too much? How can you like somebody too much?"

Rainbow Sparkle stretched out on his laptop as if the thing were her personal napping couch, and it gave Cooper an idea. "What if you learned Rainbow Sparkle wasn't really a kitten, but a baby tiger?"

Sophie laughed. "She's not a tiger."

"I know that, but let's pretend for a moment. A kitten is a very good pet for a little girl, yes?"

"The best. I love Rainbow Sparkle." She put her hands over her heart for dramatic effect.

He touched the spot where her hands lay. "I know you do. But a *tiger* is not a good pet for a little girl. A tiger could hurt you, even if you loved it very much. You'd need to think hard about keeping Rainbow Sparkle, then. You'd have to decide whether or not you could take the chance of what Tiger Sparkle—" he couldn't believe he was actually saying those words "—could do because you never really know if you can trust a tiger to keep behaving like a kitten."

"I suppose." She didn't look convinced. Cooper wasn't convinced, either. "So, Miss Tess is maybe a tiger?" His metaphor made even less sense when Sophie put it that way. He thought he'd only succeeded in confusing his daughter further until she looked up at him. "Only, you can't ask a tiger if they're planning to do tiger things, and you can talk to Miss Tess."

For a six-year-old, she had a remarkable grasp of the situation. The old "out of the mouths of babes" saying, right in front of him, twirling a strawberry-blond curl around her finger.

"I have talked to her, sunshine." He wasn't quite sure how else to put it. "I've asked her about the tiger things, and she answered me." She had. She'd answered every single question and been beyond truthful to him, laying her heart and her whole painful history out completely before him on that road yesterday afternoon.

And he'd stood there and told her he couldn't say what she wanted to hear—couldn't proclaim with full certainty that he trusted her and believed in her. Even that wasn't true. He could say it. A huge part of him burned to say it, but he wasn't sure enough and had chosen not to.

He was protecting himself and Sophie, and that was right. It's what a father does. A parent makes the hard calls for the sake of his daughter.

Only it not only felt hard, it felt wrong.

"Don't you believe her that she isn't a tiger?"

Part of him couldn't quite believe he was even having this conversation with Sophie. Another part of him thought perhaps Sophie was the only person he *should* be having this conversation with—not Hunter. He told her what he told Tess. "I want to believe her."

Sophie blinked at him as if the answer was the easiest thing in the world. "Then do."

"Tigers are big and scary. I don't want to make a mistake that could hurt you or me."

Sophie leaned very close to his face. "Daddy," she said, taking Cooper's face in her hands, "Miss Tess is a person, not a tiger." At that point Cooper was pretty sure his metaphor had gone awry, but he had to admit Sophie had a point. He'd built a career of being able to read people, and his instincts told him Tess was sincere. A bit overemotional, entirely too distracting, but sincere. Was he letting Hunter and Lynette keep him from what might turn out to be the best thing in his and Sophie's life? Yes, all the facts arrayed against her were true, and they lined up in a way that could be seen as dangerous.

Or they could line up in a way that was merely Tess. Wanting to show love and be loved.

Had he really lost his ability to tell the difference?

Few things in life were quieter than the Texas dark at two in the morning on way too little sleep. Cooper sat in his chair out on the back patio that night, staring at the stars, trying to make peace with the voice in his head that shouted, *Hunter is wrong*.

The clarity of his instincts—especially with people—was what had got him to where he was today. He could read people. He usually knew—not always at first, but almost always eventually—when owners were hiding facts, changing stories or making things up. Not that anyone ever set out to deliberately deceive the Pine Brothers, but little deceptions slipped through in the same way people weren't always truthful with their doctors. He'd had more than one physician remark how what he and Hunter did wasn't all that different from a physician's or therapist's practice.

That same instinct told him Hunter was

wrong about Tess. Granted, his brother had uncovered true facts, but Hunter assumed motives that Cooper was nearly certain weren't there.

*You know what I feel, Lord, what I sense. You gave those gifts to me. But they failed me with Lynette. What was the point of all that mess if not to make me cautious about what's happening now?*

He'd been moody and unsettled since making the decision to come to Martins Gap, even though he'd known it was the right path. That shadow had begun to lift with Tess—which made no sense because Tess made everything more complicated. Tess challenged him and pushed him and had gotten close to Sophie too quickly for his comfort. *Too close to me for my comfort.* Everything he'd told Sophie today was true, except none of it could counterbalance the void he felt in Tess's absence. It had wrapped itself around him as she'd driven away and hadn't left since.

*What if Hunter's suspicions were true? What if she really does need my money and whatever influence I have to get her out of this hole?* It didn't necessarily mean she was evil or manipulative, just desperate. After all, he knew he'd do anything—even something patently foolish—if it was desperately needed for Sophie, and that didn't make him a bad person.

Cooper realized, with a rather shocked, helpless feeling, that whatever Tess might want wouldn't undo what he now felt for her. He'd fallen for her. She'd already stolen his heart—any decision he made wouldn't make those affections disappear. He'd just have to deny them and stay unhappy for a long time—because he would be unhappy for a long time—to protect Sophie.

*But Hunter is wrong*, that voice kept insisting. *He's not wrong about the facts, but he's wrong about the woman.* He couldn't deny that Tess genuinely connected with Sophie in a way no one ever had. When he shut out his practicality, his heart knew she went too far with her affections because that was who she was, not because she needed anything from him.

The French doors opened and Glenno came out onto the patio. "The whole house can hear you thinking," he said with a wry smile. "It's always that way when you and Hunter fight."

"Hunter and I aren't fighting," Cooper replied.

"Could have fooled me," Glenno said, easing himself into the opposite chair.

"We…disagree on a crucial subject."

Glenno gave a soft laugh. "I wonder how Tess would feel about being referred to as a 'crucial subject.'"

"Am I that obvious?"

The man shook his head. "That, and Sophie is that talkative. And I walked by your office while you were explaining about kittens and tigers." He leaned in. "I know you are the animal expert, but I don't think you got that one right."

"Oh, yeah?"

"Only a baby tiger can grow up to be a tiger. And anyone with a heart and two eyes can see the difference between a kitten and a tiger cub."

"It was a metaphor, Glenno, not a zoology lesson."

"What do those famous instincts of yours tell you about Tess?"

Cooper shook his head. "Those famous instincts feel like they're drowned out by, well, other not so famous instincts at the moment."

"So you admit you care for her. Too much, as you said earlier."

There seemed little point in denying it. "Way too much."

"Did you talk to her about what Hunter found out? About what Hunter thinks is going on?"

"She admitted to everything. She's knee-deep in debt from an adoption scam back in Adelaide. She agrees she latched onto Sophie because she was hurting from the loss of that little boy. She told me she just wants to be with us, not take anything from us." He looked up at Glenno. "She just about begged me to let her into my life."

"And you said no. Why?"

It should have been a simple answer of wanting to protect Sophie. But Tess's words kept coming back to him. He ran his hands through his hair and said, "Because she scares me." He stood and began to pace the patio. "She could tell me anything and I'd believe her. I'd swallow any lie she told me just to keep her near. I can't trust myself when I feel that way about her."

Glenno stared at him. "You don't believe that. You were never afraid with Grace."

"And look what happened!" Cooper nearly shouted. "She's gone and Sophie's on crutches and someone like Lynette can slide in and blindside me because I'm still a walking wound." He stilled, startled by his own outburst.

Glenno was silent a long time before saying, "And so is she. Only it seems to me she is reaching out for healing and you are not. You are hiding behind your need to protect

Sophie, only Sophie has already let Tess in. I could say how that horse has already left the barn, but I know how you despise bad horse jokes."

Cooper threw Glenno a look.

"From where I sit, this has been a good thing. For both you and Sophie. You made friends. You went to church. You didn't hole yourself up on this ranch and keep the world out. There's facts, and then there's truth. You're making this about Hunter and his facts, but the truth is it's about you and your wounds." The man cracked a smile. "Since when have you ever done what Hunter told you to do just because he told you to do it?"

Glenno had a point. He and Hunter argued all the time. It was half of what made the Pine brothers the success they were. Neither one swallowed the other's version of things whole—they fought and struggled and beat the best solution out of each other's viewpoints.

He'd swallowed Hunter's version of Tess's actions whole, because it was less scary than letting Tess tear down the wall he'd built since Grace. The wall he'd built higher since Lynette.

Glenno pushed himself up out of the chair. "You think about that. I'm going back to bed.

There's apple pie in the fridge. If you're going to be up all night, you might as well not be hungry."

With that, Glenno left, closing the French doors behind him to leave Cooper alone with his doubts and all that silence.

# Chapter Seventeen

Tess watched as Luke poured a glass of iced tea from his fridge at the guest house. She'd finally gotten up the nerve to walk across the lawn, knock on Luke's door and tell him the whole story of everything that had happened—with Australia and then with the Pines. Everything, including the heartbreaking scene out in front of Cooper's gate. Gran was right: it was time to stop holding all of this in. She felt like she was coming apart at the seams as it was.

"I don't get why you couldn't tell me all this earlier," Luke said as he sat across from her at the small table. "You know me—I've messed up more ways than I can count. I'm in no position to judge, and I like to think I could have helped, even if it was just to be a shoulder to cry on. I know we've had our moments, but I would have been there for you."

"I was embarrassed. I made terrible choices." Tess sighed as she slumped in her chair.

"I've made dozens of terrible choices. For terrible reasons," Luke confessed. "You? You were just trying to do something good." He shifted toward her. "How much do you need?"

She told him and he whistled at the figure. It had been even higher before Gran's assistance. "I got a wedding coming up, but I can help some. Gunner and Ellie will kick in, too. You know they will. You really sold your photography equipment?"

"All but my two favorite cameras."

He raised one eyebrow. "That's not much to go on."

"Well," she told him, "it might be enough. I got an email from the magazine yesterday asking me if I'd consider an assignment in New Zealand."

He looked surprised. "You're thinking about taking it? Really?"

"It's more money than I can make here. I'll have to start paying Gran and everyone else back sooner rather than later. And…" She looked out the guest house window in the direction of Cooper's ranch. "It doesn't feel like a good move to stay here right now, anyway."

Luke gave another low whistle. "You're really hung up on him." Her brother shook his head as if the idea couldn't quite fit in there. "Cooper Pine. You always did have a knack for liking the wrong guy. Remember Jeff Nelson?"

Jeff Nelson had taken her to the prom with disastrous results. She'd had a huge crush on him, and he'd turned out to be a total jerk. Luke had left his own prom night with Ruby to come rescue her when Jeff got a bit too free with his affections and his father's bourbon. "This is different." She sighed, remembering how Luke had never once called her out for ruining his big night with Ruby. "Cooper's a good man. He's going to do great things with that ranch."

"So you believe him? That he's really going to follow through with that therapy ranch?"

Now that Hunter knew, there'd been no reason she couldn't disclose Cooper's plans for Pine Purpose Ranch to the rest of her family. They'd been surprised, but more than pleased not to have the Pine Method show setting up shop across the road. "Of course I do."

"But he doesn't believe you." Luke's tone was accusatory.

"It's not like that." Cooper had a right to be cautious when it came to his private life. She couldn't hope to understand what it was like to be in his position. At least, that was what she told her broken heart.

"Yeah, it is," Luke countered. "I'm with you—he's just telling himself it's on account of Sophie, but he could choose to believe you if he loved you."

Tess let her head fall into her hands. "He doesn't love me."

"Maybe not, but you love him. Give me at least enough credit to have figured that out." After a pause, he reached across the table and grasped her hand. "I wish you wouldn't leave. I kind of like the idea of all of us back together again." When she shot her twin a look, he added, "Yeah, I know, the last thing you'd expect to hear from me."

She smiled. "Ruby really has been good for you. She always was before, but I can see it twice as much now. You marry that girl quick before she realizes what she's doing."

"A month away," he replied, glowing.

She'd always felt Ruby was the one for Luke—much of the distance between the twins had started when he'd left Martins Gap and Ruby behind to go be a rodeo star. He'd been a rising star until an accident had ended his career. Ruby had helped him discover what really mattered.

Tess had thought maybe her return here was her own path to what really mattered, but it wasn't to be. *I hurt so bad, Lord. I can't figure out what You're up to and why all the pain. I want to trust that You have good things in store for me, but how much longer will I have to wait?* She wiped away the tear that snuck down her cheek.

"You're strong enough to stay," Luke said as he noticed the tear. "You know that, don't you?"

Leave it to Luke to find the one thing to set the waterworks flowing again. "I don't feel like it."

"Can I go yell at him? Maybe throw a neighborly punch in his direction when his daughter's not around?"

"Absolutely not!" He was kidding of course—not that Luke hadn't started his share of fights in high school when it came to defending her honor against any perceived slight—but she loved him for the sentiment. "I can't make him believe me over his brother. This situation is bigger than me, anyways. He has to decide the whole world isn't out to hurt Sophie. Funny thing is, Sophie already knows that. You saw her in church, nothing knocks her down. I've never seen a six-year-old more ready to be out in the world."

"Yeah, she's got spunk, like Gran said." Luke looked at her. "Kinda reminds me of you. And Audie. And Ellie and Gran. Come to think of it, that kid's a regular Buckton. I see why it hurts so much." He made a big show of pausing for a moment. "You sure I can't sock him just once or maybe just poke him real hard with a stick?"

"No!" Tess laughed. Luke could always make her laugh when she was down. He was right—she would have been so much better off if she'd talked to him weeks ago.

"I get that you can't stay friends with Cooper, but do you think you can stay friends with Sophie? She adores you and Audie. Audie says she's got a cell phone now—by the way, who gives a six-year-old a cell phone?—maybe you can text her or something."

"The cell phone was her uncle Hunter's idea."

"Of course," Luke said. He hadn't lost his distaste for the Pine Method franchise, that much was clear. "I won't be that kind of uncle to Nat and Nate."

Now it was she who gave him a look. "You? You most certainly will. I fear for our godchildren with you being their crazy uncle

Luke. No." She sighed again. "I don't think we'll be able to stay in touch. And I want to do something to say goodbye, something that will really last, something Cooper would allow. I just don't know what."

Luke squeezed her hand. "You'll think of something. I know you will."

It came to her in a quiet flash, the pop of an idea in her brain. It was a big risk—if Cooper thought she'd gone overboard before, he'd think doubly so if she could pull this off. But the minute she thought about it, she knew she had to try.

She looked at Luke and grinned. "I think I just did. What time is it in Toronto?"

He blinked at her. "I have no idea. Why?"

She got up from the table, leaving the tea glass half full. "I gotta go email a lady about a leg."

"I'll just pretend I know what that means," Luke called as Tess let the screen door bang behind her.

"You slept forever, Daddy." Sophie was rolling Tess's ribbon and tinfoil toy around in front Rainbow Sparkle on the kitchen floor as Cooper came in for coffee.

"I was up most of the night," he yawned.

"Working?"

"Thinking," he replied. "About kittens and tigers."

"Oh," Sophie said, giggling as Rainbow Sparkle pounced on the little silver ball. "What about kitties and tigers?"

He crouched down to the two of them. "About how they're not the same."

She looked up at them. "Everybody knows that."

"You're right. Everybody knows that." After a moment he said, "I was thinking I wanted to go visit Miss Tess this morning. What do you think?"

"Are you gonna argue with her?"

"Actually, I was thinking I might just talk and see if we can make things better between us, like you said. Want to go visit Audie?"

"Sure I do."

"Let me just send Uncle Hunter a quick email and we'll go on over."

Cooper walked to his office, intending to send Hunter an email that said "thanks for the investigation, but I'm making up my own mind," when he saw an email from TBuckton@BlueThorn.com at the top of his inbox.

He clicked to open the email, unsure of what would be inside.

It was a forwarded email attached to a message from Tess.

It's probably just more overboard, I know, but I couldn't not do this, if that makes any sense. Once I remembered JaneAnn talking about the Step Forward program, I knew it could be the one thing—the one lasting thing—I could do before I left.

Left? He knew things would be distant between them, but he hadn't figured on her leaving. And from the sound of it, it seemed like she might be gone soon. Panic pushed his pulse up as he read the forwarded message from JAKennedy@Delight.com.

Please pass this along to Mr. Pine on our behalf. I'm pleased to be able to meet your request, and I'm sure the people at Step Forward will feel the same.

The next paragraph started with the words *Dear Mr. Pine*. Clearly a message addressed to him.

We were honored and delighted to provide your Sophie with a doll. We know representation means so much for little girls, even in the world of play.

I spoke with Tess Buckton yesterday about another organization we partner with called the Step Forward Foundation. With your approval, the foundation will partially underwrite the cost of getting Sophie fitted for a prosthetic just like her doll's if she so chooses. We know it can be difficult to keep a growing girl in quality prosthetics.

On a personal note, I'm a horse owner myself and I thank you for all you and your brother do for challenged owners and their animals. I was happy to make the doll happen when Tess called—we had no idea you were the parent of an amputee daughter. Upon hearing about Sophie, the Step Forward organization was delighted to offer her a chance to participate in their program, as well. You can visit the website below to arrange for Sophie's doctor to contact Step Forward about having Sophie fitted.

Best wishes for a bright future for both you and Sophie.

Sincerely,

JaneAnn Kennedy

Vice President of Marketing, Delight Toys

Cooper didn't know what to say. On the one hand Sophie's prosthetic was a highly personal matter. A father's decision about medical care for his daughter. It *was* overboard.

But overboard was who Tess was. He couldn't ignore what an extraordinary gesture it represented. Maybe even an answer to a prayer, since this was one way to spur Sophie's enthusiasm for what he knew would be a long and challenging process. He couldn't ignore God's hand in the timing—Sophie was just beginning to recognize the things she might be able to do without her crutches, and school was looming in the fall.

"Sophie!" he called as he hit the print button and grabbed his hat. "Get ready to leave right now—quick as you can!"

"Daddy, stop ringing the buzzer." Cooper had hit the intercom button multiple times until Tess's grandmother Adele came on the line.

"It's Cooper Pine."

"Hi, Granny B!" Sophie shouted into the intercom.

"Hi, sweetie," came the old woman's amused voice.

"I need to see Tess. Now."

"She's not here, son. She went into town."

Martins Gap wasn't that big that he couldn't find her. "How long ago?"

"'Bout twenty minutes. I'd check at Lolly's if I were you. She'll be headed there at some point if not right off."

"Thanks, Adele."

"And, Cooper, son?" Her voice crackled through the speaker.

"Yes, ma'am?"

"Don't come back without her, you hear me?"

"We won't!" Sophie said, turning for the SUV. "C'mon, Dad, let's go!"

He hadn't told Sophie about the prosthetic yet—he wanted to do that in front of Tess. He wanted to do a lot of talking to that woman, but he mostly wanted to make things right. Right now.

"Look for the Blue Thorn truck," he told Sophie as they headed down Martins Gap's one main street.

"I'm looking," Sophie said from her spot in the back seat.

*I need to find that woman right now*, he prayed.

As he pulled past the sheriff's office, he and Sophie shouted, "There it is!" in unison, spying the Blue Thorn pickup parked outside Lolly's Diner.

*Where it all started*, he thought to himself. *Perfect.*

Tess walked out of the diner just as Cooper and Sophie made it to the front door. He'd had what he was going to say all set in his head, but it left him the moment he saw her. That was it. Just the sight of her—standing there holding what had to be a bag of Lolly's blondies—flooded his system with an uncontrollable glow.

Sophie had no such problem. "Miss Tess!" she yelped, wrapping Tess in a crutch-y hug. "I missed you."

*I've missed you, too*, Cooper thought. He had. Life without Tess in it felt half empty, lacking in a way he'd never have guessed. He held her eyes as he raised the printout of JaneAnn Kennedy's email. "You did this?"

She gave a helpless shrug. "Yes." He felt her standing near him, a physical sensation like the prickling of his skin before a storm, only more wonderful. "Like I said," she went on, her fingers going tight against the bakery bag. "Once I remembered JaneAnn talking about it, I couldn't not. I figured I might be able to do one last thing for Sophie before I left. If you'd let me."

Sophie tugged the paper from his hands. "Daddy, what is it? You haven't told me yet."

"It's a gift," he explained to her, forcing his gaze from Tess down to Sophie's wide eyes. 'Miss Tess talked to some people who can give you a prosthetic leg just like Molly's if you want."

"A leg?" She looked between him and Tess. 'You mean a fancy pink one like she has?"

"Or any color you want, actually," Tess said, her voice tight, like she was trying not to cry. Cooper looked up to see Tess's eyes glistening. "But I think pink's a nice choice. If your daddy says it's okay."

He could hear the nervousness in her voice and knew he'd made her afraid to be nice to Sophie. That sent an ache of regret through him.

"Can I? Then I could carry Rainbow Sparkle. And my books to school. Maybe I could learn to run. I kinda remember running and it looks like fun."

*I kinda remember running.* Cooper's heart cracked wide-open. Sophie spoke the words with no sadness, only that amazing adaptability he loved about her.

He looked up at Tess. That crack belonged to her, that wide openness right into the core of him was her doing. And so was all the love she was pouring in. If he'd suspected as much before, he knew it now. She wasn't out to get anything from him. Tess was giving. And giving and giving. And while it may be overboard, it wasn't wrong. It was everything right in his world.

He looked right into Tess's eyes as he said. "I think it's a great idea. Pink or any other color you want. And if you don't want the ones they have, we'll find you one you like." He felt his throat tighten as he added, "And, yeah, running is fun."

He reached toward Tess and the tears welling in her eyes spilled over as he grasped her hand.

"What'd you mean about before you left?" Sophie asked. "You're not leaving, are you?"

Cooper could only bring himself to mouth the word "Don't."

"I-I'm…well…" Tess began, her eyes never leaving Cooper's. "I was thinking I have to go back to where I do my work soon."

"But you'll come back, right? Like Daddy and Uncle Hunter come back?"

"I don't want her to leave at all," Cooper cut in. "Don't you think so, Sophie?"

"I don't want you to go," Sophie agreed.

"Please," Cooper managed to choke out, not caring he was about to plead in the middle of a Texas sidewalk where anyone in the world could see. "Please stay." He tightened his grip on her hand. "I like overboard. I'm crazy about overboard."

"Really?" Tess barely got the word out. Her tearful sniffle just about did him in.

"Sophie," he said, reaching for the bag in Tess's hands without taking his eyes from hers, "will you hold Miss Tess's blondies for a minute?" He handed them down in Sophie's direction, pulling Tess close as he felt Sophie take the paper sack from his fingers.

"Why? Can I have one?"

The smile that spread across his face felt as if it grew from the center of his heart. "So I can do this." And with that, he pulled Tess close and kissed her. She melted against him with a wondrous joy that spread through every part of him.

Sophie gave a startled laugh, and Tess made a tender, astonished sound as she wrapped her arms around him.

"Daddy!" Sophie giggled. "Everybody's looking!"

Cooper pulled his face back just far enough to realize he was feet away from Lolly's front window, now crowded with a collection of Martins Gap citizens in various stages of surprise and delight. One old man tapped on the window and winked as he gave Cooper a thumbs-up sign.

"Do you have any idea how invasive yo[u] are?" His tone was the complete opposite o[f] the last time he'd said those words.

Tess's smile sent his pulse to the sky. " [I] suppose I do. But it's for all the right reasons Cooper. Tell me you believe that."

"I believe it. I believe you. Stay here. Let'[s] find out what this is. Let's work through it al[l] together, the three of us. Please."

She nodded and kissed him, and all th[e] whoops and banging on the window couldn'[t] have stopped that kiss for the world.

# *Epilogue*

Tess adjusted the bright turquoise ribbon in Sophie's hair one last time. "You ready?" Sophie and Audie looked so beautiful Tess thought her heart would burst.

"We're ready," Audie said, looking down at Sophie. They each held up the basket of flowers they carried.

"Dad will have your crutches in the pew if you get tired or sore," Tess reminded Sophie.

"I won't."

"You'll be great," Audie cheered as the bridal march filled the church.

Tess looked down the aisle to see Luke standing by the altar, grinning like a fool, with Gunner beside him. Behind her, just out of sight, Ruby looked radiant in her bridal gown. *I'm so glad I'm here*, Tess thought. She nodded to Brooke, who knelt near Luke,

motioning tiny Trey forward with his rin
bearer's pillow.

Tess made a quick check of her gown be
fore sending Audie and Sophie down th
aisle.

Sophie. Beautiful Sophie walking dow
the aisle on her prosthetic, without crutche
happily using both hands to strew flower pe
als from the turquoise baskets she and Audi
carried. Her plan to get at least down the aisl
ahead of Luke's soon-to-be bride without cry
ing was lost.

Tess caught sight of Cooper, his face ra
diant with pride at his daughter's steps. Sh
saw Gran, looking beautiful and thrilled wit
all the blessings God had given her. She sav
Nash and Ellie, each with one of the twin
in their arms. Behind them, Witt and Jan
stood holding hands and looking as happ
as she felt.

*Thank You, Father, for this. For all of it.*

At the reception, Tess laughed when Rub
threw the bouquet straight at her. Her breat
caught when Ruby rushed up to her saying
"Cooper told me to."

She turned to look at him. He grinned an
shrugged. They'd talked of marriage, and sh
knew it wouldn't be long before he slippe

a ring on her finger and she'd say yes to becoming Mrs. Pine. But she wasn't awaiting it impatiently. There was no rush, only love.

"My turn to go overboard," he said into her ear as she fingered the bouquet of yellow roses. "With this." He held out a piece of paper.

Tess unfolded it to reveal a printout of an Adelaide to Austin international airfare itinerary, listing three passengers. Two names she didn't recognize. The third one stuck out like a beacon, making her gasp. She looked up at Cooper.

"Bardo and his foster parents are coming for a visit next month. You're going to be a godmother again."

"What? How?"

"Let's just say the Pine brothers know how to pull a few strings. You can't be his mom, but you can be part of his life. The agency was more than willing to cooperate once I told them the whole story. And they're also happy to help you press charges against Garvey."

"Cooper!" She kissed him, thinking if she didn't hang on to that man she might just fall over from all the happiness in this day.

"Bardo can come back for the wedding, too, if you want."

She smiled at the gleam gathering in his eye. "Which wedding?"

"Ours." He grinned. "But that's a conversation for another day. Right now I want a dance with the most beautiful lady in Texas." His grin widened. "And after that one dance with Sophie, I want ten dances with you. Every day. For about fifty years."

As she gazed after him on his way to Sophie, Tess felt a tug on her elbow.

"Did he just say what I thought he said?" Gran whispered.

Tess felt as if she glowed. "I think so, Gran."

Gran hugged Tess. "If there's a happier place in the world right now than the Blue Thorn Ranch, I don't see it."

Tess hugged her right back. "Me neither, Gran. Me neither."

\* \* \* \* \*

*Don't miss these other*
**BLUE THORN RANCH**
*stories from Allie Pleiter:*

*THE TEXAS RANCHER'S RETURN*
*COMING HOME TO TEXAS*
*THE TEXAN'S SECOND CHANCE*
*THE BULL RIDER'S HOMECOMING*

Dear Reader,

The Bucktons have become like family to me. I've had such fun bringing each of the four siblings and their cousin home to the love and faith of the Blue Thorn Ranch. I hope when I am in my eighties that I have the strength, wit, faith and gumption of Grannie B. It's my prayer that these characters have become as dear to you as they are to me.

If this is your first visit to the Blue Thorn, please go back and enjoy the previous stories: *The Texas Rancher's Return*, Book 1, *Coming Home to Texas,* Book 2, *The Texan's Second Chance*, Book 3, and *The Bull Rider's Homecoming*, Book 4.

As always, I love to hear from readers. You can email me at allie@alliepleiter.com. When you visit my website at alliepleiter.com, click on the Contact tab to sign up for my newsletter to hear about all my upcoming books and events. If social media is your thing, you can find me on Facebook, Twitter and Pinterest. If you prefer regular mail, you can reach me at P.O. Box 7026, Villa Park, IL 60181.

Blessings,
*Allie*

# Get 2 Free Books,

## Plus 2 Free Gifts—

### just for trying the Reader Service!

LIS17R

# Get 2 Free Books,
## Plus 2 Free Gifts—
just for trying the
### Reader Service!

◆ HARLEQUIN®

## HEARTWARMING™

**YES!** Please send me 2 FREE Harlequin® Heartwarming™ Larger-Print novels and my 2 FREE mystery gifts (gifts worth about $10 retail). After receiving them, if I don't wish to receive any more books, I can return the shipping statement marked "cancel." If I don't cancel, I will receive 4 brand-new larger-print novels every month and be billed just $5.49 per book in the U.S. or $6.24 per book in Canada. That's a savings of at least 19% off the cover price. It's quite a bargain! Shipping and handling is just 50¢ per book in the U.S. and 75¢ per book in Canada.* I understand that accepting the 2 free books and gifts places me under no obligation to buy anything. I can always return a shipment and cancel at any time. The free books and gifts are mine to keep no matter what I decide.

161/361 IDN GLWT

| | |
|---|---|
| Name | (PLEASE PRINT) |

| | |
|---|---|
| Address | Apt. # |

| | | |
|---|---|---|
| City | State/Prov. | Zip/Postal Code |

Signature (if under 18, a parent or guardian must sign)

### Mail to the **Reader Service:**
**IN U.S.A.:** P.O. Box 1341, Buffalo, NY 14240-8531
**IN CANADA:** P.O. Box 603, Fort Erie, Ontario L2A 5X3

**Want to try two free books from another line?**
**Call 1-800-873-8635 today or visit www.ReaderService.com.**

HW17